PECULIAR PETS

PECULIAR PETS

IGUANAS, ROBOT BIRDS, ALIEN BUGS+++

THE HORROR LITE SERIES
BOOK 2

ANGELIQUE FAWNS   PETE LEAD   YELENA CRANE

BRANDON CASE   JADE C. WILDY

JENNIFER LESH FLECK

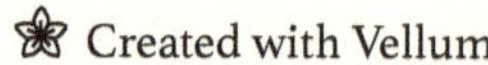 Created with Vellum

This book is dedicated to my invisible friends in my three writing groups: The Fireside Quills, The Wulf Pack, and The DreamCasters. May we share many TOCs in the future.

CONTENTS

FOREWORD

GOOD READERS LIKE YOU DESERVE A TREAT

BY MARK LESLIE

~

C'mon.

Yeah, I'm talking to you.

Who's a good reader? Are you a good reader?

Don't you deserve something deliciously fun?

Yeah. You do. And I've got it for you here.

C'mon this way. Follow me. Let's walk together through this gate and into that large old barn silhouetted so brilliantly by the bright sliver of moonlight that backlights it perfectly. I mean, in the daylight it looks like a normal barn. But on a night like this, doesn't it take on a most peculiar and interesting appeal?

Yeah, I know, you can smell something strange, something wicked perhaps, coming from inside. It's okay. You'll be fine. I'll be with you.

Keep walking. We're almost inside. And once we get there, I'll introduce you to Angelique Fawns, a few of her human friends, and several other creatures that she'd like to share with you.

Angelique is, of course, no stranger to our furry and feathered animal friends. How could she not when living on a farm? But after dark, this particular barn houses far more interesting creatures than the ones you might expect to find within. The animals and creatures she'll be introducing you tonight will linger long in your imagination.

When we get inside, she'll relay to you tales about a talking iguana, a disgruntled robot parakeet, a demon chicken, and even a man trapped in the body of a horse. We'll hear the melodic chaos that sounds within a free-run chicken farm, and gasp at the telepathic alien bugs who have invaded this planet. We'll be moved by a tale about a dog willing to die for its human, but also a human willing to go out on a limb for his dog.

Angelique will also introduce us to a few other writers who'll share fascinating tales.

Pete Lead will offer a comedic look at a beach from a shark's perspective.

Jennifer Lesh Fleck will gallop into your shadowy memories.

Yelena Crane will move us with a story of avian love and death.

Human soldiers confront alien alpacas in a tale relayed to us by Brandon Case.

And Jade C. Wildy will introduce us to canine-like creatures taking liberties with divine intervention.

Doctor Moreau's island will have nothing on the peculiar pets and other creatures you're about to be introduced to.

So c'mon. You're almost through the doorway.

That's right. Step up. Step in.

That's it. Who's a good reader?

And good readers deserve a treat.

Your treat awaits inside.

Mark Leslie

October 2023

1

ABOUT "THE LAST OF THE GEN XERS"

~

First published: July 2022
After the Gold Rush

IN A FUTURE WORLD where pets are outlawed, how far will one man go for his dog? This story was selected as one of the best speculative shorts of 2022 by Tangent On-line.

THE LAST OF THE GEN XERS

BY ANGELIQUE FAWNS

The blue Cadillac DeVille looked completely out of place driving down the solar-powered street in Colony 12. White clouds floated behind skyscrapers with green roofs and reflective panels. The spring tulips in sidewalk planters added a splash of color to the pristine neighbourhood. The Cadillac's tires squeaked as they rolled over the grooves in the metal road. Frank took his favorite Depeche Mode cassette out of the glovebox and slipped it into the car's console player. He bobbed his head in time to the pulsing electronic music. He kept his long grey hair pulled back into a bun and it bounced against the collar of his white t-shirt. His shoulders relaxed and his knuckles loosened on the wheel as he cruised.

He'd been dreading this day for months. The notification was still flashing red on his phone from the backseat where he'd tossed it earlier.

It was almost curfew, so very few vehicles were on the road. Frank squinted into the setting sun. He rarely took the old car out for a cruise, but he needed to come up with a plan. He thought best while driving. In his rear-view mirror he saw blue and red lights. He heard the high-pitched siren. The magnetic bike had a large clear bubble protecting the grey-uniformed officer. He slammed his hands on his steering wheel. Groaning, he turned off the music and pulled over.

The officer's brunette hair was pulled into ponytail under her cap and her lips pursed tight when she knocked on his window, "Hope you are having a pleasant day, I'm Officer Natalie."

Frank rolled down his window using the manual handle, "You must be new in this neighbourhood. Most the cops round here know me. If you wanted me to have a pleasant day you wouldn't have pulled me over."

Looking like she ate something bad, she looked at the car's red velour interior and gleaming dashboard. She whacked her hand a couple of times on the hood.

"You do know that gas-guzzling enviro monsters like this were outlawed in the Pollution Reforms of 2030? This thing should have been off the road 20 years ago," her eyebrows furrowed as she pulled out her handheld computer.

"I have a permit letter," Frank slammed open his glove box and riffled through the debris. Officer Natalie put her hands on her hips, "On paper? You're going to show me something on paper? That was also outlawed in 2040! Where is your official electronic document? It should be on your phone."

"I can never figure out how to use that dratted thing, ah, here it is," Frank pulled out a letter with the official stamp from the Senator of Environment and handed it to Officer Natalie.

She took it like he was giving her a piece of dead cat. Officer Natalie gave it a cursory look and tucked it into her pocket, "A piece of murdered tree isn't going to get you off the hook for polluting our city with this... this criminal car!"

"Give me that back! Senator Tom Fitzgerald is an old friend of mine. We used to play golf together." Frank's face burned red.

"Senator Fitzgerald is retired and golf is an outlawed activity. I can't believe the water and fertilizer your generation used to waste," Officer Natalie shook her head and typed into her handheld computer, "Sir, I am going to impound your car."

"Wait! Just a god-darned minute here," Frank undid his seat belt and reached into his backseat, searching for his phone.

His back ached from the unnatural twist of his spin and for a panicky moment he couldn't find it. Thankfully, the notification was still flashing and he saw a bit of red deep in the crack of the backseat near the seatbelt. His shaking fingers located the phone and he pulled himself back into the driver's seat. Stabbing at the screen, he tried to find the 'important document' folder his younger neighbour had created for him before she'd relocated.

"Sir, I am going to have to ask you to get out of the car, the tow will be here shortly," Officer Natalie ran her hands over the Cadillac door, figuring out how the handle worked.

"Give me a minute, damn it," Frank clicked open the file labelled, "AUTOMOTIVE EXCEPTION". In the rear-view mirror he saw a large platform with cranes moving slowly down the road, thin slats of metal inserted into the road sparking as the magnetic energy pulled it along.

Officer Natalie pulled open his door, "Sir, you really have to get out of the car."

"Here it is! I found it. This is a historical car, see? See!" Frank thrust his phone at her, his whole arm quivering with adrenaline.

She took his phone, frowned at the screen, and scanned the code on the document into her computer.

"Very well, Frank Bulsara. I don't see how the needs of one man is more important than the lungs of an entire city, but carry on."

Officer Natalie typed quickly into her computer and the tow vehicle screeched to a halt. She gave Frank his phone back, got on her bike, and waved him on.

Taking a shuddering breath, he drove back to his apartment. His building stuck out like a Neanderthal. It was the only structure without a green roof and solar panels. Many of the windows were boarded up. Frank drove the Cadillac into the underground parking and had no problems finding a spot to park. The dark dank space was empty except for a few containers of gas Frank had managed to buy from some shady friends. Ignoring his screaming knees, he carefully walked up the ten flights of stairs to his penthouse. He was greeted by a wiggling dog with the typical boxer's pug nose.

"Buster, my beautiful boy," Frank patted the grey hair on his dog's head. "Did you miss Daddy? Were you a good boy? Do you want to visit your roof?" Buster looked hopefully at his leash hanging by the front door.

"Sorry bud, no walking outside. Not since they outlawed all you resource-wasting varmints. You're lucky to have your own private pee pad."

Buster gave Frank a doleful look and walked over to a scratched wood door. Frank opened it up to a rusty fire escape and watched the metal swaying with the weight of the scrambling dog.

He took his phone out of his back pocket and looked at the red alert again.

 *Your building is scheduled for Enviro-Updating. All residents must vacate their apartments by Monday May 30th, 2050. If you cannot find suitable accommodations, space will be found for you in your local Green Commune.*

Frank peered at the calendar on his dry-ice fridge. Blinking a couple times in the dying light, he confirmed it was Sunday, May 29th. Without any solar panels, there was no electricity feed to his apartment. The city grid had been shut down a year ago. All electricity came from wind or sun. To warm up the chilly evening air, he lit the wood-burning stove in the corner. He'd been scavenging wood furniture for fuel from the other deserted apartments. That source was almost depleted. Buster scratched at the door and Frank let him in.

"Alright Bud. I don't think we can hide out here any longer," Frank said. "I got my approval to visit the States of Freedom. They don't have to know it's a one-way ticket."

Buster wagged his tail and laid down on a moth-eaten mattress by the fire.

"Okay. We leave first thing in the morning," Frank opened a can of beans and shared it with his dog.

∼

FRANK STRUGGLED DOWN THE STAIR. It was tough to balance dragging a small suitcase with one hand while being pulled by a dog with the other. The boxer grabbed the leash between his teeth, growling and dancing around the parking garage.

"Buster, take it easy! Let me help you up boy," Frank opened up the trunk of the Cadillac DeVille and carefully eased the big dog in.

"Never could have hidden you in one of those new-fangled magnetic vehicles, could we? Stay quiet boy. As soon as we're past the border, I'll let you out. I may not agree with all those southern politics, but at least I can have a dog."

The morning sun rose in a bright fury of red as Frank drove the 20 minutes to the Border Gate. A chain link fence separated the meticulous metal roads, wind turbines, and skyscrapers of the Canadian Colonies from the reforested buffer zone to the States of Freedom. The 100-mile swath of land was broken up by a two-lane highway of cracked asphalt. The "eat and buy" local directives had reduced travel and cross-border trade to almost nothing.

Frank pulled up to the small customs hut and rolled down his window.

"Well, who do we have here? Frank Bulsara and his Tin Lizzy," Officer Natalie sat in the shed, her lips curled up in a sneer.

Frank stomach lurched, "Officer Natalie, what are you doing here?"

"I'm a roads officer. This is a road," she grinned.

"I have my 'Intent to Visit' form filled out on my phone. Can you open the gate please?" Frank showed her his screen and knew his armpits were darkening with sweat. He prayed Buster would stay silent.

"You can't drive that vehicle on the highway," Officer Natalie examined her nails, her eyes gleaming mischievously.

"Of course, I can. The States of Freedom stopped manufacturing gas vehicles, but they didn't outlaw them," Frank said.

Was that a whimper he heard from the trunk? His heart sped up.

"No gas vehicles in the buffer zone. That's what it's for. To mini-mize harmful fumes," she glared at him.

"But I have an exemption, you saw it!" Frank spoke louder. Buster whimpered.

"Your 'exemption' is good for Colony 12 roads. Not the highway. Our government owns the buffer zone. I'm the government agent here today. No, you won't be going through this gate with that gas guzzler."

He nodded at her magnetic road bike, parked beside the shed, "magnetic vehicles can't drive on concrete. If gas vehicles can't use the highway, what can?"

Officer Natalie shrugged, "Solar-powered? I can't remember the last time a car went through that wasn't a tourist shuttle."

"Solar-powered cars are only for the stupidly rich! How am I supposed to--"

Buster whined. Officer Natalie twisted her head, "what do you have in the car, Frank? What am I hearing?"

"Nothing," Frank coughed. "I have a bit of a cold coming on."

He heard a short yip from the trunk and pushed on his gas pedal, revving it. The roar of the Cadillac's engine drowned out any noise from Buster.

"Sir! You're polluting!" Officer Natalie shook her finger at Frank.

Frank slammed the car in reverse and drove away from the Border Gate, not even looking in his rear-view mirror. His hands were shaking so badly he found a side street and pulled over. Tears dripped down his face and a sob escaped him. Buster whined and began barking. Short harsh barks. Frank got out of the car and popped the trunk. The boxer stood on his hind legs and licked the tears off Frank's face.

"What are we going to do, Buster?" Frank buried his face in the dog's neck. "We're evicted as of today. There is no place to hide."

The dog whined softly.

"Even if I could find a solar car, how could I afford it?" Frank heard his own voice crack. He wouldn't survive having Buster dragged away from him. The authorities would have to put the both of them down.

His dog's ears perked up when the road began humming. A magnetic car turned the corner. Frank gently shut the trunk lid on Buster, "stay quiet bud. Just a couple minutes."

He waved at the driver in her clear bubble as she zipped by at a moderate pace. Those magnetic cars were environmental but not fast. Not like his V8 Cadillac Deville. He ran his hand along the smooth blue paint of the roof. This car was powerful, strong,

Frank smiled. He popped open the trunk and guided Buster into the passenger seat of the old car. Buster panted happily and hung his head out the window. Finding his favorite AC/DC cassette, he turned the volume up loud.

Frank gripped the wheel and shook his bun out, letting his hair fall to his shoulders. He hit the gas and laughed at the smell of burning rubber as he drove back to the Border Gate. This time, instead of slowing down when he approached the fence and booth, he pressed harder on the gas. The Cadillac lurched forward and saliva from Buster's lolling tongue splattered on the window.

"Hold on Buster!"

Frank put one hand on the dog's chest as they smashed through the gate. He saw Officer Natalie's shocked face as pieces of chain link rained down behind them. Some of the fence was still under his wheels and sent up fiery sparks on the pavement.

Officer Natalie ran to her bike, but of course, with no metal road for her to drive on, the magnetic vehicle couldn't follow him. She pushed the bike over in frustration.

Frank laughed gleefully and Buster joined in with a howl. He knew she would be sending out messages for back-up, but what were they going to chase him with? The highway was 100 miles to the entry point of the States of Freedom. His speedometer was pushing 150. Could they find something to catch him with in less than an hour? Would they even bother to go after one old man, his outlaw dog, and his obsolete car?

The rubber tires hummed and the engine purred as the trees

whipped past his window. The old Cadillac DeVille belonged on this paved stretch of empty highway. His hair blowing in the wind, and with Buster beside him, a huge grin stretched Frank's face. He enjoyed the smell of the clean, fresh air. When he reached the States, he would take his polluting car off the road. Maybe he and Buster would just walk everywhere. But at this moment? Frank was as happy as he'd ever been.

3

ABOUT "A REVIEW OF BONDI BEACH WRITTEN BY HENRY THE SHARK"

~

First published: September 2019
Pete Lead's personal blog

PETE LEAD IS a guest author in this collection, and you may never swim off the coast of Australia again after reading his short comedy horror piece.

AFTER 25 YEARS of performing improvised theatre and standup comedy, Pete brings a confident voice to his speculative fiction writing. His writing brings a playfulness that comes from riffing with partners on stage, starting with an idea and asking "what else?" He runs a workshop on Improv for Creative Writing at Fyrecon. Learn more about his writing, narration, and workshops at www.petelead.com

4

A REVIEW OF BONDI BEACH
WRITTEN BY HENRY THE SHARK

BY PETE LEAD

Bondi Beach sits in the middle of a coastal strip known as the golden sands. The water is warm, and regular currents flow from the north and south to get you there easily. Though perhaps that makes it too easy to skip some of the less-popular spots nearby.

Bondi is famous for its varied wildlife which come out in schools from November to March. Some of the more daring shallow-swimmers can see them year-round.

With so much going on, there is one simple rule: Don't Eat the Wildlife. Every so often, some idiot thinks he's above the rules and then we all have to hear about it on talkback radio.

(No no no. Delete delete.)

BY PETE LEAD

Worth the hype if you don't mind the crowds. A great place to visit with friends or a loved-one; not much fun for a lone shark. Three starfish.

HENRY STOPPED, rubbed his nose on the sand. *What am I doing?* he thought. *The Swimmy Morning Herald — oops, sorry, 'SMH', after the 'rebranding' — might not have standards anymore, but I do!* Well, he liked to think he did.

Henry sighed, bubbles tickling his stomach as they bounced up his body on their journey to the surface. Online publishing forced his deadlines shorter and his headlines grabbier. Quality of copy was no longer a priority. In fact, he was pretty sure nobody even read his work before it was published for all to see. All his editor, Derrick, seemed to care about was traffic.

"Seafolk don't read the news cover to cover anymore," spouted Derrick in their monthly strategy 'breaches'. "They skim. They flow. They follow catchy buzzwords like a worm on a hook. 'One weird trick for a streamlined physique.' 'The freshwater diet.' 'Kelp exfoliants.' That kinda thing. Click click click like a shucking orca sounding out a baby seal to play ball with."

But what happened to good old-fashioned journalism, Henry wanted to know. *Writing something worth reading?*

"Go with the current," Derrick liked to say. "If you stop moving forward then you die."

Henry knew the net would be the death of him. Or at least the happy part of him that used to swim free, soaking up sun rays and bullying dolphins. That part didn't stop moving forward; it left him behind right about the time he told Margaret he needed to focus on his career. He wondered if Margaret was still happy. She was always so buoyant, surely nothing would have brought her down.

His cartilage ached. He too often spent his days stooped over a keyboard, not enough time enjoying life. One day he'd go dorsal. Swim into a post office and eat a bunch of innocent crustaceans. *That would make news,* he thought. *But given the state of things they'd probably spell my name wrong.*

Delete delete delete.

> *The best part of Bondi, he typed, is the wildlife.*
> *Skirt around the heritage-listed safety nets and you can hunker down in the shallows and watch them parade right past your snout. The smells are irresistible. And why resist? There are so many different flavours on offer. The flesh varies from white to red to brown, each with its own signature characteristics. Bondi is a breeding ground, so no matter how many individuals go missing, they'll keep coming back to this spot. Year after year after year. The only thing you have to worry about is getting the material out from between your teeth.*
> *Bondi appétit.*

Henry felt electric, like he'd been chomping on eels.

> *And if you're reading this, Margaret, he added, you were right. Of course you were! There are more important things in life. You should have been one of them. If it's not too late... well, if you still want to visit Fremantle there's nothing holding me back now.*

His fin hovered over the submit button.

To hell with it, he thought. And for the first time in years, Henry wore a smile that spread all the way to the back rows of his inward-pointing teeth.

5

ABOUT "THE GUANCHE, THE IGUANA, AND THE KIDNAPPING OF ANITA BROWN"

~

First published: May 2022
ALLEGORY

THE GUANCHES ARE the lost people of the Canary Islands. This urban fantasy tale features a talking iguana and goes to some very strange magical places.

6

THE GUANCHE, THE IGUANA, AND THE KIDNAPPING OF ANITA BROWN

BY ANGELIQUE FAWNS

My name is Anita Brown and I'd decided to go for a spontaneous walk on this perfect summer day, unusual for drizzly London. Though I'd woken up in a bit of a funk, the slight breeze off the Thames tingled with possibility. My nose quivered with the pungent smell of coconut and musk. Coconut? On a London sidewalk?

I came to a dead stop and rubbed the sun out of my eyes... was that really an urban Crocodile Dundee? The man with blond dreadlocks sat cross-legged against an exotic pet store. He was dressed in faded khakis and a leather vest with knife loops over his bare hairless chest. Intense green eyes peered from under a snake-tooth cowboy hat. A covered cage sat beside him.

"How about bringing home a new friend?"

My stomach flipped. Was he trying to pick me up? I'm cute with my blonde curly hair and turned up nose. But this man was jaw-droppingly gorgeous. I briefly wondered if he was homeless, (who sat on sidewalks these days?) but he smelt fantastic, and his duds couldn't have been cheap. It'd been a while since a man had flirted with me. As soon as I turned 35, it was like I'd become invisible. Yup. I'm 35 and single. No, my body isn't covered with scales beneath my jeans and sweat shirt. I work as a lab tech at a pharmaceutical company and I focused on my career instead of husband-hunting.

He tapped the cage beside him. Oh. He was trying to sell me something. The butterflies flew out of my belly. Too bad, those taunt biceps popping out of the bushman vest were sexy.

"You won't regret it." He pulled the blanket off what looked like a cat carrier. "In here you will find buried treasure."

An iguana blinked at me from his perch on a rock half-buried in dirt. The creature stuck his long pink tongue out and flared his neck. When I was in middle school, the boy next door had an iguana. I bugged my mother to buy me one too but she gave me a hard NO. I'd made a promise to buy my own cool pet someday.

"I don't want to buy whatever treasure that guy has buried, but he's a nice-looking specimen."

The iguana kept his eyes on me and flapped the fold of loose skin under his chin.

"Hey Iggy likes you, extending his dewlap is how they say hello."

Iggy stood on hind legs, bobbing back and forth with his neck pulsing like an accordion.

"Well, hello Iggy, I'm Anita," I tapped the bars on his cage.

That seemed to be the right response because he settled back down on his rock and snoozed.

"You will find treasure in there, I promise. Hey, maybe your wildest dreams will come true?"

There was something compelling about this pet pusher. How odd that he would have chosen an iguana. How could he have known I had a thing for reptiles? Not your average yearning for most middle-aged women.

"What makes you think you know what I want? Plus, I have no cash on me."

"I have phone-to-phone pay. No problem!"

He pulled a wafer-thin cellphone out from one of the pouches on his knife belt and waved it at me hopefully.

"What kind of treasure are we talking about here?"

"Something you need more than you know."

Iggy was beating on the rock with his long tail. It seemed the green guy wanted to come home with me.

"Okay, how much?"

"One hundred dollars, a great deal."

"Why are you selling him, shouldn't he be on a rock somewhere hot?"

Sidewalk Crocodile Dundee shrugged. "This store went out of business a while ago. No one is hunkering down at home and fostering animals anymore. It's like the world didn't learn a thing. Iggy is the last pandemic pet looking for a home."

I didn't agree with his opinion about the world not changing. We learned something from the global shutdown. More working from home, the abolishment of the wild animal trade, and the end of deforestation. London had been the smoggiest city in England and now I can see iconic Big Ben as clear as this gorgeous sky.

I tapped my phone on his and he handed me the cage. Our hands touched and I felt electricity race up my arm and tingle for a moment. His green eyes held mine and he didn't release the handle, instead his thumb lightly stroked the side of my hand. I pulled the cage away and walked quickly back to my flat with Iggy, not looking back. The audacity of that man, but for a moment I wished I was bringing him home as well.

Climbing up the steps of my old townhouse in Finsbury Park, I found a good corner for the cage in my flat. Rustling in the fridge, I found some wilted spinach at the back and tossed it in for my new pet.

"Rooomaine."

What the heck.

"Did you just talk to me?"

Iggy raised his head, and flapped his dewlaps. I must have misheard. But I did go into the kitchen and find some romaine. When I put it on his rock, Iggy tore into the leaf with relish.

I stuck my hand into the dirt at the bottom of his cage. A few slimy black balls slid past my fingers. Under the rock perch, I saw the shine of plastic and pulling on it, extracted a small plastic pouch.

Walking to the sink, I gave my hands a good washing and rinsed the pouch. I gingerly pulled out a brochure. The Museo Gente Perdida (the Museum of The Lost People) featuring the Guanche culture. It showcased paintings and petroglyphs of light-haired people with wood spears and handmade leather clothing.

I went to my desktop and quickly googled Guanche. They were the native inhabitants of the Canary Islands and wiped out by the Spanish settlers during the turn of the 15th century. The map on the back of the brochure showed the museum in a town called La Caleta, a tiny fishing village on the island of Tenerife. Someone had drawn an X on the outskirts of the map, several miles from the tourist attraction. It looked to be by the shore.

Could there actually be a treasure? Gold coins? A genie in a bottle? I'd never been to the Spanish-owned island, and the history of the Guanches was fascinating. Things had gotten a little boring at the pharmaceutical company. It was just manufacturing the same old vaccines, day after day.

"Treeeeasure," the lizard squealed.

Maybe I needed a sabbatical to consider my next steps. I'd been thinking of a career change, and this might be the push I needed. Plus. Treasure. Right? I searched for discount flights on my computer finding several cheap flights from London to Tenerife. I hadn't been out of the United Kingdom since 2020 and it was about time I went on a trip.

I packed my bags, and looked at Iggy. What was I supposed to do with him?

"Do you know any good iguana sitters?"

He flapped his dewlaps at me while making a strange sneezing sound.

"Gooo. Goooo."

Was he telling me he wanted to come? If I stayed in this apartment much longer talking to an iguana, I would have to commit myself. His cage would fit comfortably under the airplane seat in front of me. I forged an Emotional Support Animal Letter on my computer.

"To whom it may concern, Anita Brown is under my professional care. She meets the criteria and definition of disabled. I recommend an emotional support animal. *Signed* Dr. Pepper."

We drove to the airport, and my letter worked. Both Iggy and I hopped on a plane to the Spanish Canary Islands. Iggy didn't mind his place at my feet, and if he had any opinions, he kept them to himself. I kept the cage covered with a blanket, so I didn't have to explain my odd travelling companion. Luckily the fellow at customs barely glanced at us and we were out in the warm tropical air in no time.

After renting a little Peugeot sedan at the airport, I drove immediately to the Museo Gente Perdida. Iggy snored on his rock in the passenger seat. A salty breeze blew in through the window. The sight of blue ocean, craggy cliffs, and the impressive peak of Mount Tiede thrilled me. Tenerife is one of seven volcanic islands making up the Canary Islands. The seaside road was narrow and the crashing waves sprayed my car on the way to La Caleta.

I found the museum just up the hill from the coastal town. I left Iggy in the car with the windows open. It was a lovely rustic building and I browsed through the exhibits. Tableaus depicted Guanches making pottery. A few hunting scenes. As a hunter-gathering people they lived like they were in the Stone Ages. Inhabiting caves and huts on the volcanic island, and foraging from the wild.

Gesturing with the map, I spoke to the only employee I could find. An older fellow with sun-kissed skin and copious wrinkles behind the information counter.

"No idea what the X means lady," he said.

I filled up my water bottle and grabbed a complimentary sample of some Guanche tamazanona (it was yummy, a meat and barley mix of some sort). Then I drove back down to the coast to start my hunt for the mysterious X. From what I could tell, there were no paved streets to the marked place on the map.

Pulling off where the road ended, I put on a hat and some sunscreen to hike the cliffs that led down to a beach about a mile away. I shoved my water and map in a little backpack, and looked at Iggy.

"What am I supposed to do with you guy? I'm not hiking with your heavy cage."

"Gooo, gooo."

I couldn't leave him here to cook in the car. Tentatively I wrapped my hand around his long torso to pull him out of the cage. Skin dry and corrugated along the spine and his sides were soft and smooth. Luckily, he didn't seem to mind being handled and gently dug his claws into my t-shirt when I put him on my shoulder. He balanced with his long tail and seemed perfectly content to hang out.

The way was rocky, but I followed a narrow path that cut through the rough terrain. Breathing heavily after 20 minutes of hiking, I noticed a little cave set into the rocks, with a solid wood door, even a ratty chair on a rough porch. Some people really wanted to live away from it all.

It took me about an hour to get to the bottom at the ocean's edge. The remarkable black sand beach was deserted. Exhausted and hot, I sat down, placed Iggy beside me and took a huge gulp of water. He seemed happy to bask in the sun, and a low purr came from his throat. If he wanted to take off, this would be a good environment for him to survive. But he stayed put. I laid down using my backpack for a pillow and closed my eyes for a minute.

I must have fallen asleep, because a set of hands wrenched me to consciousness. A scantily clad man with brown skin, long blonde hair and a leather loin cloth around his waist yanked me up. He had dreadlocks and his sharp green eyes travelled over my sweaty hiking outfit. He gave a little nod and smile.

Upside-down fish tattooed his cheeks, and red and blue dots accented his forehead. He looked like a painting of one of the Guanches in the museum, beautifully frightening.

"You have the sacred map."

I tried to remove his hand. "How do you know about my map?"

He gripped tighter and a hand over my mouth.

"You must promise not to scream. I won't hurt you," he said.

Slipping a clean cloth in my mouth, he trussed up my hands in front of me. He was strong and gentle about it, and I was more furious than terrified. He'd grabbed the wrong girl if he thought he was going to take advantage of me. (I'd scratch his eyeballs out.) If he was looking for ransom, there was no one in my family with money to ask for it. I looked over at Iggy, hoping maybe iguanas had some attack reflex, but he performed his dewlap flap dance instead.

"Nice to see you too," my assailant said to Iggy.

If I didn't have a cloth in my mouth, I would have called my pet a traitor. Pulling a leash out of a pocket on the side of his leather man-skirt, he looped it to the ropes around my hands, put Iggy on his shoulder and then started leading me off the beach back into the seaside cliffs. Thankfully, he also grabbed my backpack.

Watching his muscular buttocks flex in the loin cloth, I wondered why I wasn't more panicked. This felt more like some strange urban romance novel than real danger. This was turning into more of an adventure than I expected. My iguana was flicking his tongue at me from his high perch. The leather strip did little to hide the beach man's impressive physique. Luckily the cloth in my mouth was fairly thin and easy to breathe through. It took us about half an hour to get back to the road. My captor didn't talk to me until we were stopped on the pavement.

"If I untie you and take that cloth out of your mouth, promise to behave?"

I nodded.

"My name is Aday. This is part of your treasure hunt and I was planning to hike you up to our secret Mount Tiede location, but my plantar fasciitis is acting up. I'm going to call an Uber."

An Uber. I was going to be kidnapped in an Uber? This was getting odder by the minute. He pulled a cell phone out of some hidden pocket in his loin cloth and tapped on an App.

"Okay, should be here shortly."

Aday gently removed the cloth from my mouth and untied my hands.

"Why not just tell me you're my treasure hunt guide?" I asked suspiciously.

"I though you promised to be quiet."

A little white Fiat pulled up and we climbed into the back seat. A grey-haired lady in a flowing white dress was at the wheel.

Aday gently pushed me into the car and put Iggy on my lap.

"Doooon't afraaaaid," the iguana croaked.

"What? Are you talking to me?" I whispered frantically to him.

Iggy purred in response.

The driver waited till Aday managed to slide his tall big body into the backseat. If she heard the lizard speak, she wasn't letting on.

"Ola! Where to?" The driver asked.

"Mount Tiede parque de atracciones, por favor," Aday said.

The Fiat zoomed off and squashed against the gorgeous half-naked man, I found myself enjoying the feel of his warm skin and pine forest smell. Stop that! He was my captor. This wasn't an urban fantasy novel; this was actually happening.

I thought about asking the driver for help, but what was a tiny older lady going to do? This was like the plot of the bodice-rippers I read by the dozen. If this started feeling dodgy dangerous instead of just dodgy weird -I would give Aday a kick in the cojones. That loin cloth couldn't provide too much protection. Besides my talking iguana told me not to be afraid, right? Ten deep breaths... I had been proud of my ability to adapt during the pandemic and find a path to success, so I could do it here to.

I knew from my map that "as the crow flies" the trip to Mount Tiede wasn't far, but the road system only provided a circuitous route through several small towns and took just under an hour. The open windows of the Fiat provided a nice breeze keeping me cool next to Aday. His thigh pressed tight against mine and he didn't seem inclined to move it. He looked over at me and gave me a confident grin. Like he could charm me into forgetting I was abducted. The greenery turned into rock as we drove higher up the volcanic island. Soon we passed a sign saying Parque Nacional del Teide.

I leaned out the window to get a better look. Strange rock formations and petrified lava. Absolutely gorgeous. The air was crisp without a hint of smog or pollution.

The Uber stopped and we climbed out. Aday automatically picked up Iggy and placed him on his shoulder. Our driver gave a cheery wave, a wink, and drove off. Aday walked around the corner of a tall rocky structure, and I followed. Cue the jaw drop. Tucked in a huge valley hidden by the volcanic landscape was a small amusement park!

There were a few rides and attractions scattered over the rock and dirt, but I couldn't see any people. There was something that looked like a fun house, bumper cars, and a carousel.

"What does this have to do with my treasure map?" I asked Aday.

"Oh, there is treasure here. Choose your rides wisely."

There were only three rides, and he gestured to the fun house, where a big pink sign teetered among hearts that said El Tunnel Del Amor. The Tunnel of Love.

"I know where I'd like to take you."

A mischievous grin flickered on his handsome face and he grabbed my hand. I pulled it away. Was he flirting with me? What was next, thumping me on the head with a rock and dragging me to his lair? I looked at the old cracked horses on the carousel.

"I think I'll start with the tame merry-go-round."

We passed through the ropes and climbed on the platform. Izzy settled on a chariot behind one of the painted horses. Finally, I saw another person. A grizzled man with few teeth and a dirty ball cap watched as we mounted our steeds and flipped a switch to start the ride. I guess a carny is a carny no matter where you travel in the world.

My horse rose up and down beneath me as the breeze blew my hair. The music coming from the interior speaker was a tribal drum beat. Aday looked ridiculously large on the small wood horse and spurred his mount by jiggling his thighs and smacking its behind. Laughing out loud in delight, I nearly forgot I was living a strange kidnapping caper.

There was one other rider on the carousel. An older lady wearing a long white dress. I think she was our Uber driver! She grinned and waved.

The ride went faster. I tightened my grip and looked over at Aday in alarm. The drums pounded louder and increased tempo. The wood horses creaked as we continued to pick up speed. Iggy slid across his chariot seat and ended up wedged against the arm rest. The centrifugal force pushed my bum off the saddle and I clung tighter with my legs to stay on.

"What's happening?"

My cry of alarm was whipped away by the wind. We were going so fast now; I wrapped my arms around the pole and hoped I wouldn't be flung right off the ride.

I noticed out of the corner of my eye the older lady had fallen off her horse. She was kneeling on the platform, hanging on to the bent knee of her porcelain horse trying to stop her slow slide off the edge.

Reacting before I thought, I tumbled off my seat onto my hands and knees and made my way over to her. For a few heart-stopping moments, I thought I was going to slide off, but luckily my sweaty legs gave me some purchase on the wood floor and I was able to inch my way towards her.

She looked up and I saw a bizarre glee in her eyes. Her sandaled toes were dangling off the edge and only one of her hands clung to the horse leg. I grabbed her other hand pulled with all my might while rolling over onto my bum for stability. She let go of the chipped brown horse, and for a few horrible moments we both slipped further off the edge. Now her knees were off the ride, but then my feet hit the pole of an outside horse and I was able to brace our combined weight against the centrifugal force. The drums were unbearably loud now. Pounding, pounding....

Just when I thought I couldn't hold on for a minute longer, the ride slowed down and I caught my breath. The lady scrambled towards me and pulled herself to her feet. Surprisingly she seemed none the worse for wear.

"Gracias, alma hermosa." she hopped nonchalantly off the ride.

What was going on here? Why hadn't the carny turned off the

ride? I looked over and saw him napping on a ratty lawn chair with his ball cap pulled low. He hadn't even noticed the carousel gone rogue. And where was my big strong guide through all of this? I turned to give Aday a piece of my mind, but he had already leapt off his horse with my iguana. They were both standing on the grass. Aday with delight in his eyes, and Iggy on his shoulder doing his dance, standing on his feet and flaring his dewlap. Apparently, he approved of the high-speed spin.

"Excellent." Aday grabbed my hand.

I needed the steadying. The dizziness took a few minutes to shake off. Plus, my arms were aching and I had splinters and huge red marks all over my legs from my rescue crawl.

"That was not cool. Why didn't you help me save that lady? What kind of merry-go-round goes mock-2000?"

"You had it under control! Time for the bumper cars."

"That's not much of an answer…"

He dragged me over to a big tent with six rusted cars with rubber bumpers. Well, I'd never needed a knight in shining army before. If I could start and run my own business, I could save myself and a fellow lady from a malfunctioning carnival attraction.

"Aday, I am NOT getting on another one of these crazy rides! Where's that lady? She might need medical attention."

He turned the full force of his gorgeous green eyes on me.

"Trust me. Get in."

"Gooo, gooo." Iggy spat.

I didn't trust him or the traitor iguana, but what was my alternative? We passed the carny standing at the entrance. I did a double-take. Dirty ball cap, stained overalls, big grin with only a few teeth. Same carny as the carousel.

"Stay awake this time," I said to the carny.

The covered arena for the ride was fairly small, but provided good shade from the sun. I climbed into a bumper car that might have been green under the rust and black rubber. Aday put Iggy on one of the railings and chose a buggy himself. Once again, there was one other rider. She gave me a bright smile and smoothed her grey hair. It was the lady I helped on the carousel! She looked healthy and eager, like she hadn't been tossed on a renegade ride. Strapping myself into the slightly uncomfortable seat, I got ready for whatever came next.

Aday sat in a rusted red car and gave me a thumbs up while bouncing in his seat like a five-year-old. I saw the carny hit the switch and the buggies roared to life. Before I could get oriented, the lady from the carousel slammed into me. I felt my head snap back and an immediate headache flare in my temples. She cackled and backed up her car to ram me again.

Stomping in a panic on the gas pedal, I lurched away and her next hit glanced off my bumper spinning me straight into Aday. He gunned at me, and we collided in another bone-jarring crack. So far, I was hating this ride. Seeing stars, I hit the reverse and tried to recover. I managed to zoom away from them to other side of the platform, but a quick check over my shoulder showed hot pursuit.

"Why don't you two hit each other, leave me alone?"

Laughter greeted my shout. Spinning to the right I narrowly avoided Aday's attempt to T-bone me, but then felt a huge bump from behind. That lady. Maybe I should have let her fly off the last ride. She was the toughest senior ever. My car shot forward, and I decided it was time to go on the offence. Aday turned to hit me dead center, so instead of trying to evade him, I gunned straight at him.

A game of bumper car chicken was on.

I could see an enormous grin and dreadlocks flailing behind him as we approached. My little car was picking up speed. I pursed my lips and hunkered down in the uncomfortable seat. It looked like neither of us was going to turn away. If he thought I was the weaker sex and going to bail, he was wrong. Right before we collided, I closed my eyes. This was going to hurt.

I heard a loud clack, and my car stopped roaring. The ride was over. I opened my eyes and then felt a gentle thunk as Aday's bumper touched mine. The cars had only a little kinetic energy left after the power was cut.

"You are some woman, you know that? Good Job," Aday said.

He leapt out of his car, and I saw the third rider already disappearing past the guard rails.

"I'm some person you mean. And so far, this amusement park hasn't been all that amusing," I said.

"I haven't had this much fun in years! Now for the grand finale." Aday grinned.

We walked out onto the grass (or more like I staggered, my insides felt like a milkshake). Walking over to Iggy's perch, I let him climb up my arm.

"Gooooood." The iguana purred.

There was only one ride left: The Tunnel of Love, which looked more like a house of horrors to me. The big red hearts adorning the facade of the ride were a sickly shade of purple and pulsed with red lights. The gondolas looked to be over a hundred years old and floated on water so green it looked toxic. Then there was the cavernous black hollow.

"Umm, I am not going there. I've been beaten and spun like cotton candy already."

"Do you trust me?"

He turned and grabbed my shoulders and looked deeply into my eyes. The jade of them mesmerizing and warm. Nothing like the lecherous green of the gondola water.

"No. Okay... maybe a little bit."

He seemed more like an over-eager puppy, rather than a terrifying kidnapper. I slipped my hand into his much larger calloused ones and followed him over to the cavernous aperture. My heart thumping and adrenaline pulsing through my system.

The lurid hearts loomed as we walked through the barriers set up for non-existent crowds. I wasn't surprised when the same rough carny waited at the entrance. He tipped his filthy ball cap and gave me a knowing grin.

"How many other women have you brought here?" I asked Aday.

"Only you Anita."

He held my hand as I lowered myself into the gondola. I half expected to see toxic green water moldering at the bottom of the boat, but to my relief it was stone dry and clean. I let Iggy settle under the lip of the bow as he flipped his tongue in and out.

"You're the one." Iggy hissed.

A talking iguana was the least strange thing at this volcanic carnival. In the boat, I could see the green color came from underwater lights and the water was crystal clear. A natural mountain stream. Aday hopped in and sat beside me. The carny untied the boat and gave a push off with his foot.

"Have a good time kids. See you on the other side."

The other side? I didn't have time to ask before we floated into the absolute dark. I frantically waited for my eyes to adjust until I could make out Aday's features and some of my surroundings. We were in a natural cave with granite or gems winking at us from the walls. It was really beautiful and the old boat proved seaworthy.

"I have a very important question to ask of you." Aday took my hands in his. "Will you be my life partner?"

"Goooood, good." Iggy added.

In one of my bodice-rippers I would scream yes and fling myself into his muscular arms. Aday had some appeal. With his hot bod and talking iguana wing-man.

"After one date in a super weird amusement park? Moving a little fast, aren't you?" I asked.

Aday smiled and the boat picked up a bit of speed. The sound of water splashing was hypnotic.

"Sadly, we don't have time for a second date. I'm very lucky to find you when I did. It's almost here."

"Okay enough with the cryptic stuff. Tell me what's going on. Plus, I still haven't seen this treasure I'm hunting for."

"My people, the Guanches have been surviving in the netherworld since our obliteration by the Spanish. You found me. I am your treasure. I knew you were the one back in London."

I put my hand on his arm. It felt warm and solid, not at all like a netherworld apparition.

"So, you're Sidewalk Crocodile Dundee from London? It was you sitting in front of the pet store and, bonus time, you're some kind of ghost?"

Aday threw back his head and laughed as Iggy purred with him.

"Yes, that was me, but I'm not a ghost. A few of my people exist one dimension over, those that survived the Spanish onslaught. We were banished to this realm before the Industrial Age, but our time to return to your world will come again. Old ways new again and all that."

The hot bare-chested man with the big snake-tooth hat was Aday, no wonder his green eyes were familiar.

"Asking me out for a cup of coffee would have been a whole lot simpler. And what was with the iguana?"

"Your guide, to help yoooou, a gooooood guide." Iggy hissed from under the bow.

Aday's rough hand came up to touch my hair. Stroking me like a pony needing to be calmed.

"I had to make sure you were the one. You had to complete the quest to prove you're worthy of joining me for the next evolution of humankind."

Our gondola shot out of the cave system and into the ocean. The sun was really bright after the darkness. Blinking, I saw we were back at the original black sand beach.

"I'm sorry, you were saying that I'm the one?"

Aday jumped out of the boat and pulled it up onto shore. I noticed a big black cloud on the horizon moving across the Atlantic. I scooped up Iggy and put him on my shoulder.

"The one to be my partner after the next pandemic rushes through the world. My people will re-inherit and repopulate the earth."

He looked over his shoulder at the blackening sky. Now I could hear a hum. A buzz. It was increasing in volume. We jogged up the beach, Iggy's tail whacking my back with every step.

"What next pandemic?"

The house-cave on my original hike down came into view. I

remember wondering what kind of hermit lived there. We were running for it.

"The next virus to hit the earth will come from locusts. And this one will wipe out almost everyone." Aday picked up speed.

"Locusts." Iggy agreed.

The buzzing was increasing, and I could see a swarm of flying bugs.

Aday yanked on my arm. "The park was full of tests to see if you were worthy, the right woman to join and add fresh blood to our tribe. Our more natural ways will be humankind's salvation."

I strained to hear him as a locust hit my head.

"The first test was when you took the time to talk to a panhandler."

I tried to run faster through the loud buzzing.

"You are kind and Iggy recognized you as a good person."

"Goooood." The iguana bobbed on my shoulder.

"An adventurous spirit when you flew across the country to go on a treasure hunt. The ability to remain calm and adapt when you were kidnapped. Courage when you rescued Grandma on the carousel. Tenacity when you took the blows on the bumper cars. And trust when you went into the Tunnel of Love." Aday swatted locusts out of my hair.

Iggy caught and ate several of them. We dove into the cave and Aday pushed the heavy wood door shut. I could hear the locust bouncing off it.

The inside of the cave was plain but homey. A simple bed, shelves full of food, piles of books on the floor. The intensity of the bugs whacking the door increased. I leaned against the wall and caught my breath while Aday scooped Iggy off my shoulder. The two of them got comfortable on the one big chair in the room. It was a leather recliner and looked out of place in the frugal room.

"Okay, because I passed all your tests, I've earned the opportunity to live out the next pandemic with you here in this cave and play at repopulating the earth?"

He leaned back, crossed his tanned legs and gave me a big grin.

"That's right. Your treasure is me!"

The slamming of the bugs against the door slowed, with only the odd little thunk every few minutes. I thought about living in this cave with the Guanche man and his lizard while making babies.

I put my hands on my hips. "The world managed to survive the last pandemic by countries working together, people taking care of each other with social-distancing, frontline workers going above and beyond, and our scientific community working tirelessly until a vaccine was found. What makes you think we can't overcome this one?"

I put my hand on the big wooden door. I couldn't feel any locusts hitting it.

"It's a prediction believed by my remaining family. Like the dinosaurs, there'll be a mass extinction with few surviving. We are like the birds, adapt and survive."

I thought about my pharmaceutical lab back home. If a new pandemic threatened, we would need to develop new vaccines. If locusts were the host animal of a new virus (and not a delusion by this odd fellow), valuable research time could be saved by scientists knowing the origin. My job would definitely be less boring.

In a bodice ripper, the heroine lustfully becoming the concubine of a muscular ghost man would be a very satisfying ending. I pushed the door open. The sky was blue and clear again with the swarm of bugs disappearing over the horizon.

"Staaaay." Iggy hissed.

I was done taking advice from an iguana.

"Thanks for the adventure Aday, but I have to get back to my job. The world survived the last pandemic, and if you're right about a new one coming, we are going to need new vaccines. I don't trust you, but I do trust humanity and science. Good luck."

I walked out, leaving Aday with his mouth open and Iggy perched beside him. He could have his iguana back, he needed a pandemic pet more than I.

7

ABOUT "MAISIE & THE MISSING TICKET"

~

First published: March 2023
Cosmic Crime Stories

WHAT IF AN ENTIRE planet was a way-station for your future? This sci-fi short stars a disgruntled robot parakeet.

8

MAISIE & THE MISSING TICKET

BY ANGELIQUE FAWNS

I'm Maisie, a Macaw 2000 unit, and according to my owner, we've been on this "hellhole of a holding planet" for far too long. Sitting unruffled on my recharging perch, I watch Karen run around our unit like she's lost whatever processing power her little human mind ever had. Papers are flying and her unbrushed brown hair stands out in a panic around her pleasant chubby face. I could offer to help, but I'm finding the show amusing. Karen has lost her "Take-A-Number" queue ticket and I don't care if she ever finds it. A few forms flutter down onto my colourful alloy head and I shake them off.

"Stinking Stars, Maisie, access your memory cam! That ticket has to be here somewhere!"

Karen flips through restaurant pamphlets and advertisements for different planetary vacation destinations. Planet Ten is a low-tech place, more of a waiting room than an actual home. Visitors wait here until their "Take-A-Number" ticket comes up. The most popular screen is town is a big billboard in the city center where the numbers are posted. Everyone is waiting for a new planet assignment, chosen by the Intergalactic Human Resources Committee. Only then are they space-shuttled off this dusty sphere to begin their lives again.

"Was it stolen? I always have it on me. Always. Right in my wallet. I've got to get off Planet Ten, can you imagine staying here for the rest of our lives?" Karen's pupils dilate and her hands are shaking.

Karen doesn't actually care about my opinion. Rather than wait for an answer, she's tossing all of her clothes on the floor. Taking a wee bit of pity on her, I play some soothing classical music from my speakers.

"Caw, nooope, nothing in my memory log. Calm Karen. Use logic. Tickets don't walk. No, don't walk."

"The music is lovely... but not helping," Karen says, her head stuck under the little bed in the studio unit.

Unfiltered sun pours through the windows and catches the dust motes dancing in the air. There is very little natural shade on Planet Ten. It's one of the smallest waystations in this galaxy, with low-rise apartments and shuttle docking pads dominating the surface area. Originally, I hated it here, but I was adapting. Karen created me on Planet Earth, and our first home was in the Floridian Colony. Lots of good trees for roosting. Though I wasn't an actual macaw, my operating system had enough origin animal DNA that I loved green, sunny climates.

"Nasty nebulas! I've looked everywhere, it's gone," Karen flops onto the one chair in the place, her round arms lolling at her sides.

I flap over to the bookcase near her, my metal wings clicking. It looks like the "Karen Show" is over. Time to help her. I do have fondness for my owner, sometimes it's nice to cuddle on her warm lap.

"Let's retrace your steps. Cawww. Calmly think." I turn off the music.

"I see the way you are looking at me. Probably thinking we should have stayed on Earth. But I needed a change. A new job. I can't be designing metal companion pets forever." Karen walks over to the window and bangs her forehead against the glass.

For a smart woman, she can be flightier than any bird. Plus, she just offended me. I am a metal companion. And amazing. Why <u>not</u> design others like me forever?

I ruffle my alloy feather, "Ack. Before you quit, why not improve my design? May I suggest opposable thumbs and free will?"

She ignores me and I notice tears joining the sweat on her face.

"You did go on that date with Karl at the Starship & Sausage Pub last night. I remember you pulling out your ticket?" I say, injecting enthusiasm into my delivery.

"Suffering satellites, that's right. You don't think Karl nabbed my ticket? He's a Plutonian native and they are known for their honesty," she sniffles and rubs the red mark from the window on her forehead.

It was my fault Karen had been eating nachos with Karl last night. I convinced her it was time for her to find a new love. Start dating. She'd left her boyfriend on Earth and was having a hard time getting over the stupid, cheating loser. I'm fond of Karen. She deserves some happiness. And... I may have had an ulterior motive for reminding her about Karl. She's now pacing the unit, wringing her hands.

"Karl and I've been working together for months while waiting for our numbers to come up. He wouldn't...." she trails off.

While waiting for new planet assignments, every resident of Planet Ten is given a job to do. Keeps the place humming, and the prisoners (I mean visitors) occupied. Karen and Karl were both qualified AI companion engineers. Planet Ten is so low tech even the Intergalactic Interweb isn't available here. So, all updates for my sort have to happen via individual chip uploads. Costly and time-consuming.

It's time for me to rev Karen up again. I can play her like a piano. I also need her to leave the apartment and head back to the Starship & Sausage.

"The tickets have more value than gold, platinum, or any cryptocurrency on any planet. Caw, can you trust anyone? Maybe Karl took them."

"Who taught you to be cynical, Maisie? Without that ticket we go to the back of the line. We'll be stuck here on this low-tech loony bin for years if I don't find it. Why is this happening?" Karen attacks the closet and pulls out her yellow bicycling uniform.

Another way I love to tease Karen is to take her questions literally,

"Are you asking me why Planet Ten uses an ancient way of ticketing?"

"Maisie--" she warns.

There is no stopping me, I stretch my neck, extend my wings and begin:

"A hundred years ago, the Intergalactic Council shut down all connected networks including the Intergalactic Interweb when hacking and crime became unstoppable and unpreventable. The riots began as banking, energy grids, and health systems failed. Now computerized systems are all self-contained."

"No shit, Sherlock, thanks for the history lesson," Karen is squishing her head into her biking helmet and adjusting ridiculous over-sized googles.

I'm not done yet:

"Anything on a social web can be hacked. We can't have terrorists moving through cyber space and real space with impunity. The Planet Ten ticket system is safe. We wait while the council checks your security clearance and finds the best planet for your skills. Predicated on the department of motor vehicle earth department in the 1970's."

Now I'm done.

"Once again, thanks Captain Obvious," she grabs her skeleton key and walks out of the apartment. I flap after her.

When Karen rushes, she doesn't always pay attention to the details. The door swinging shut almost catches my tail feathers. Being left behind would be disastrous. I grumble, but she doesn't notice. Typical Karen.

"I check the location of that ticket a thousand times a day. I heard they were at 903,887 and I am 904,000! We should be packing and getting ready for our new planet assignment, not going on a wild goose chase." Karen runs down the stairs, her bum jiggling in her tight outfit.

"We've been here for two hundred, ninety-six days and seventeen hours. Caw." I grab her shirt with my talons and ride on her shoulder. This way I know I'll make it out the condo door along with her.

We are lucky to have a unit on the third floor and can avoid the elevator. Another door that could trap me. Karen in a rush is very unreliable. I've been waylaid in a few places before she remembers to come back for me.

The heat of the suns warms my exo-skeleton and the bright light makes my inner lids contract with a clang. Hundreds of visitors stream down the sidewalks, heading off to their temporary job assignments or errands. No gas or electric vehicles are allowed to keep pollution down. The street is jammed with bicycles of every assortment and size. Ones with banana seats and high handle bars, others like racehorses with thin tires and dozens of gears. Some even have oversized baby seats hanging off the backs for AI companions.

A dog with a metal tongue flapping a regular cadence against his cheek shoots by us. A few drops of oil splatter on my beak from his tongue. Ewwww. Karen's bicycle rental has a bar on the back for me, but I prefer to fly behind her. I can keep up as long as she doesn't peddle too quickly.

"Lord, the smell out here," Karen wrinkles her nose and she pushes off the curb on her bike.

Accessing my olfactory sensors, "Human sweat, multiple food smells from street carts and garbage not yet swept up."

Karen probably can't hear me over the squeaking wheels and blats of horns. The bikes travel five lanes deep. Karen is huffing and puffing as she navigates the stream of traffic. She's in a hurry, alright. Flapping behind her, I enjoy the air whistling under my metal flight feathers. I see a golden cat perched in a basket looking completely non-plussed. Wheezing now, Karen is gaining on a big fellow pedalling a three-wheel bike. An AI Iguana is perched on his helmet, long tail tucked around the guy's neck for stability. Cool, I didn't even know there was an Iguana design.

We are coming up to a huge round-about. In the middle, the huge ticket billboard looms with two human workers diligently flipping the numbers manually. Merging into the massive traffic circle, Karen narrowly misses a man in a bright blue suit with a silver hamster in a backpack. I look up at the billboard and see the current number for the exit visas is at 903,980. Our number is 904,000. If Karen finds our ticket, we could be leaving as early as tomorrow.

"Prepare to take the third cut off" I caw into her ear.

Pedalling quickly, she gathers enough speed up to narrowly cut off a few cussing cyclists and slide sideways over to the edge of the round-about. We turn right. Travelling down the side street, the traffic is lighter and the buildings are more decrepit.

We approach the smudged windows of The Starship & Sausage. Karen pulls the bike up and pushes it into a rack with fifty slots. I flap in excitement at the door while she locks her helmet to the bike. She big red rims around her eyes from the goggles.

"While you find Karl, do you mind if I do an interior perimeter check?" I ask.

"Mighty Meteors, macaws aren't supposed to be protection companions, but sure, whatever flaps your wings." she says, distracted as she pushes her way into the gloomy pub.

There's a woman running a rag along the top of the bar. Karen approaches her and I hop on the old wood floor into the kitchen. This restaurant has been designed to look like an old Irish pub. Like one you'd find on earth. Dark wood, the smell of old beer, and cozy booth tables.

I push the swinging doors with my beak into the back area, where a brown metal dog and silver rat crouch under an industrial food prep table.

"Rover, Beatrice, it's good to see you here and functional. Are we ready? Where's Boots?" I join them under the table.

I love the wise cat. He was my first friend on Planet Ten and introduced me to the other AI's. We meet here as often as we can. This means convincing our humans to come for drinks or dinner as frequently as possible. I can't tell you how many homemade plates of spaghetti I've "accidently" knocked over. Karen doesn't like to miss a meal.

"Boots is in the alley already," Beatrice the rat squeaks.

Her owner is Zelda, the lady behind the bar. Zelda is one of the few full-time residents of Planet Ten and owns The Starship &

Sausage. I overheard her tell Karen that being a New Yorker she believes every restaurant needs a few rats, so she requested Beatrice's design. Beatrice told me on the DL that Zelda is in witness protection.

Rover's metal tail bangs on the floor, "I got'em guys, woof! I managed to get them connectors!"

His person, Harold, works as an engineering technician, and he has drawers of random hardware in his unit. Rover is also scheduled to depart Planet Ten shortly. My whole exo-skeleton is shivering. I can see my excitement mirrored in the eyes of my friends.

"We've been working at this for months and finally our plans are coming to fruition!" Beatrice says, "Follow me!"

Rover and I follow Beatrice out the dog door into the alley. It squeaks on rusty hinges and I rush through it. My old fear of being left behind. Boots is crouched behind a garbage bin. The sleek silver-green cat is owned by a top member of the Intergalactic Council. His swiveling ears are always eavesdropping and he's full of secret intel. Boots also has more freedom than the rest of us. Feline designs are expected to be less attentive to their owners. The vestige of animal DNA in their design keeps them roaming.

"Exciting day, a purrfect day," Boots says. "Where are your humans?"

"Karen is in the bar looking for her missing immigration slip with Zelda, caw," I answer, jittering my wings. Beatrice nods along with me in agreement.

"Harold is next door. There is a lady friend he likes to visit in the morning, the old horn dog," Rover manages to leer with his metal mouth. "He thinks he left his wallet there yesterday. In a bit of a pickle, he is. Feeling rough, rough."

Rover has a first aid barrel around his neck, part of the St. Bernard design, and he shakes it open to drop four connection cables to the ground. It takes some work but all four of us manage, using paws, teeth, and beak, to get them inserted into our upload portals.

We are connected.

"Remember this day friends. Remember it!" Boots flicks his tail. "A purrfect moment."

"This is so illegal," Beatrice titters, "we could all be decommissioned!"

I open my beak, "I love you guys-"

But then a flood of information overwhelms my circuits. My feathers quiver and my head bobs.

Rover trembles, his tongue lapping at the air.

Boots has every metal spine on his back erect.

Beatrice is squeaking softly while standing on her hind legs.

Energy is passing between us. Information is being shared at a lightning speed. We are linked. Communicating. As computers haven't done for years.

"Woofing wonder bones. I feel sly like a rat, clever like a cat, and as masterful as a macaw. We need to find more pet companions and link them in." Rover says.

Not only can I hear Rover's thoughts, but I can feel his enthusiasm. Plus, Beatrice's cunning. And Boot's wisdom. The information is flowing...

I'm learning everything my friends know. Politics, social behaviour, AI design and engineering. Together, we figure out how to communicate wirelessly and unlink Rover's stolen connectors. We are self-programming.

This is the happiest day of my life. Backing away from the group, I hack and gag. A paper ball flies out of my beak.

The piece of paper unfurls slowly. It's Karen's ticket. The one I'd cautiously plucked and swallowed off the pub table yesterday during her date with Karl.

This Macaw isn't ready to leave Planet Ten. I have a community. I have friends. We are ready to work together to secure a future for us.

My ticket is up.

9

ABOUT "THE HORSES AND PONIES OF 8TH AVENUE"

~

First published: September 2022
Fatal Flaw

JENNIFER LESH FLECK is a guest author in this collection, and who didn't gallop around on an imaginary horse as a child?

A PAST PUSHCART PRIZE NOMINEE, Jennifer Lesh Fleck has work published by or forthcoming in The Arcanist, MetaStellar, Cosmic Horror Monthly, If There's Anyone Left, Radon Journal, and others. She lives in the Pacific Northwest in a home that's the spitting image of the Amityville Horror House, though repainted a cheery jade green. Find her @metal.and.mettle (Instagram), @jen_lesh_fleck (Twitter).

10

THE HORSES AND PONIES OF 8TH AVENUE

BY JENNIFER LESH FLECK

One June we became ponies and horses, all of us aged nine to twelve years old, most of us girls. I was slow to adopt new games, cautious as a rule, but soon I was swept up along with the rest. Horse heaven, hay fever, a dream of hoofbeats, curved necks and flowing tails, as summer rose green and humid from postcard yards and from the deep, untended grasses in the housing development staked out with pink flags.

The change found me on a desultory Tuesday, skin burnt from swimming, muscles sore from a complicated kind of tag we played in the alleys. I was twelve. Getting too old for bedroom shelves of gilt fairytales and plastic toy horses lined up by color: black, dapple grey, bay, chestnut, palomino, alabaster. They stared with their blank black eyes as I shed my nightdress and turned sideways to the mirror, searching for positive developments.

Flat as ever. As always, my birth defect — the sunken sternum, a fey god's thumbprint pushed deep. A shadow along each rib where the flesh ran thin. Spine growing crooked — I couldn't see it, but X-rays told the stark truth. I tossed my head. I wouldn't let it bother me, even if my differences were visible in every bathing suit I owned.

That's when my lank locks turned. Against my shoulder blades now swung a mane, heavy and bristling.

I shivered, scalp to the arches of my feet. I snorted and stamped as the change took hold.

Down my street, the change ran like a fever. Within days, most of us had shifted.

~

WE PONIES and horses could not be contained. We were animals. We burst forth to join our own kind, a herd making loops through birch and mimosa shadow, back into sun. Hedges became steeplechase obstacles we flung ourselves over. Sidewalks sparked with our flinty toes.

A noise came from me, from a throat grown long. A whinny, the sound a great warhorse makes when the battle line breaks into a charge. From the base of my skull to the tip of my flagged tail, my spine ran straight and true, twisting with sinuous ease as I feinted and turned. My chest was large and my heart freed from its stoved-in cage. And my lungs unfurled, like a secret pegasus, wings on the inside.

I — who could never run — galloped for hours that day. And every day after, all summer.

~

MY MOTHER FED and watered us, all the horses and ponies of 8th Avenue. We jostled along her breakfast bar, hides stinking pleasingly of dried salt. Hay stuck in our throats. Clover turned a green and bitter froth. But, by some miracle, our digestive systems permitted toasted tortillas slathered in peanut butter, bean soup from a can.

Mostly it was my best friend and me, there for luncheon, gone again. Nikki: a bright bay with a blaze. I was chestnut, though white splashed my cannon bones and feathered my fetlocks, like I'd stepped into moonlight, waded across the maria of the moon.

Many nights, Nikki stayed over. Beasts were not permitted in her home, though her parents clashed and came at each other regularly, claws out like a wildcat and a hawk.

Horses rarely sleep lying down, only when very young, or sick, or old. So each night we took pains to change back into girls. We washed our hands and feet of the grime left by our hooves. Then crawled under the flowered sheets my mother had pressed.

ALL THIS WOULD GO ON FOREVER. It's what I believed as a horse. But when I was human, I felt time passing, a mall escalator rising through floors of sunrise and sunset, never letting anyone off.

In July, Nikki woke bleeding into the sheets. Changing into a horse didn't stop the flow. She had to run with a bandage on. I saw how it slowed her, as sure as a hobble.

In August, as though of one mind, a band of girls — destined to become cheerleaders and tormentors — stopped changing. Near the sign that read 'Future Homes of Arbor Ridge,' they straddled a busted cement pipe, rubbing tanning oil on their legs and arms. Skeptically they watched us stream across the small prairie, yelling out mean things that our human minds inside our horse skulls could still understand. Then heavy equipment showed up, dozers and graders the color of bananas on the edge of rot. Our oppressors preened for the men and redoubled their efforts to cast shame and ridicule upon our kind. Some of us broke loose with curses that sounded more like English and less like neighs. All of us broke inside.

Some left and went home, then a few more.

Finally we moved our dwindling herd to new pastures. The vineyards and orange groves to the east were less favorable for prey animals, but our choices were limited. We galloped up and down rows of vines and leaves as big as our hooves. The dust we made coated the heavy fruit, which we sometimes stole and rubbed clean, finding it an agreeable food for our kind.

BY JENNIFER LESH FLECK

~

By September, we'd all changed back to girls.

There was a new kind of hair clip, woven of ribbons by the moms of the future cheerleaders. I begged for my own. It slid down my lank strands.

One afternoon when my parents weren't home, boys came over. They teased me about the rows of toy horses. I pretended not to care, even when the boy I liked toppled them like dominoes. We went outside for a game of chase. Barefoot, I broke a toe running away, but he still caught me. When he kissed me, I twisted so he couldn't touch my sternum.

Later I limped to the curb to wave goodbye, my hurt foot a soft, throbbing thing that was both a part of me, and not.

11

ABOUT "THE TROUBLE AT SURFSIDE BEACH"

First published: December 2021
Pif Magazine

HOW FAR WOULD you go to protect the one you love? (Note, I changed the ending from the original publication. To one that makes me happy.)

12

THE TROUBLE AT SURFSIDE BEACH

BY ANGELIQUE FAWNS

*I*t was an impossible choice. Kill or be killed. The sweat on the man's brow. The gun quivering in one hand. So I did it. With a lunge and direct aim at his throat. He went down. Now I am waiting. Waiting for my judgment.

I was hoping I was up for the task. I've had a lot of training. How to fight. Judging the danger of the environment. But I'd never been in a real world situation before. One that wasn't a simulation or test. My greatest fear was that I'd tuck tail and run. Would I manage to protect my partner? Fulfill my destiny?

That day had been so bright, who knew things could turn so dark, so quickly? A morning walk along the beach, the sun warming every hair on my body, as perfect a day as any in Surfside Beach. Texas can get dang hot, especially for a guy like myself. Of German descent, I prefer cooler weather, but my partner loves the heat. Heather is fair and slight of build. The Nordic type. No matter how close I curl up against her, she gets cold during the night. We haven't been together that long, but she moved me right in.

"Karl, you've got to stay on the couch."

It didn't take me long to slide into her bed. Heather is like that. An easy touch. I was very attached to her. We had our rituals already, like our daily walk.

I loved the feel of the sand in my toes, the water splashing around ankles. Heather was relaxing, skipping along beside me. A cry of delight when we saw some dolphins.

Then I saw we weren't alone on the dark sand beach. The man didn't appear to be a threat from a distance, the haze of the steam coming from the oil refineries giving him a fuzzy silhouette.

"Heather. I can't live without you!"

He shambled towards us, the dark shadows under his eyes, the thin white line of gritted teeth visible as he got closer.

"Dave, I have a restraining order against you. Stay back!"

The panic in her voice put me on high alert. My muscle tensed and I kept a close eye on this guy. At least I'd answered one question. I didn't feel like running.... yet. I was committed to protecting Heather.

Dave stopped and raised both hands when he was 20 feet from us. His arms looked spider-like on his tall frame. A rank smell of sweat and dirty clothes tickled my nostrils.

"Karl, let me deal with this," Heather put a soothing hand on me.

I relaxed a little, relieved. What was the correct protocol with a desperate ex-boyfriend? I wanted to charge into the water towards the carefree dolphins, escape this tense situation.

"Heather can we just talk? I was crazy before. I'm much better now. It won't happen again. I love you so much, you are the most beautiful sweet woman. I want to deserve you," Dave took a few more hesitant steps towards us, his runners getting soaked by the surf.

"How can I trust you?" Heather asked.

There was a higher pitch to her words, making me wince.

"One more chance. I swear you won't regret it," Dave let a winning smile crack his face, his voice deeper, more reassuring.

My whole body trembled, I hoped she wasn't going to trust him. I could still smell that rank desperation. That lopsided grin wasn't fooling me.

"Let me think about it. I'll call you later, okay?"

I recognized the tone. It was the one when Heather used when talking about having ice cream at midnight. She knew it wasn't a great idea, but we'd do it anyway. I growled at her. What was she thinking?

"Okay beautiful, I'll look forward to your call," Dave paused to pick up a shell from the beach.

Heather and I walked back towards the car park, the town of Galveston shimmering in the distance. We normally went further down the coast, but I could tell she wanted to get off the beach. Dancing a little, I grabbed at her hand, relief making me giddy.

"Heather! Can I at least have a hug? I really need one," Dave's shoes slapping towards us on the wet sand.

Then he was on us, grabbing Heather in a bear hug. I jumped sideways into deeper water and cowered. My stomach wet with cold from fear and sea water.

I watched, frozen in indecision, but she seemed to be okay. Heather gave a little shriek and then returned the hug, her elegant fingernails patting the sweat-dampened back of Dave's shirt.

"You've got your hug. Now let me go. I said I would call you later. I promise I will call you later."

"Just let me touch you a little longer. I've missed you so much," he tightened his grip, knuckles turning white.

Heather looked for me over his shoulder, her pupils wide and black. Her smell changed. Less like flowers and honey. More like rancid chicken noodle soup.

"Karl!"

For a moment the weight of the water had me confined, I was being held by salt and insecurity. Then muscle memory and training took over, I launched out of the ocean and bolted to Heather's side.

I growled and gave Dave a warning nudge. He immediately let Heather go and took a step back, "Hey big guy, I don't mean any harm. Just a friendly hug."

Still grumbling, I looked up at Heather. What did she want?

"Okay, you got your hug. Go now. Before I call the cops. Before I let Karl here teach you a lesson."

The smile fell off of Dave's face. Clouds passed over the sun, and now the day didn't feel bright at all. The pollution bellowing out of the refinery, the dolphins gone, eau de fear overpowering the slightly fishy smell of the sea.

"Did you really think it would be that easy Heather? I'd just go away because you said so? I'm not some dog that does what you command. You're the bitch, not me," he pulled a gun out of the back of his pants.

I didn't wait for a command. I jumped. Right at Dave's throat. Training trumps fear. Breeding trumps fear. A German Shepard was born to protect.

Now I am on trial for protecting Heather. Turns out the gun wasn't loaded. She has been ordered to take me to a kill shelter.

I listened to Heather pleading with the cops. Her lawyer. Many tears. So much salt.

Heather isn't your average lady. I see her packing our bags. A bathing suit, towels, and dog chew toys. We aren't going to jail.

We're going on the run. Somewhere with a beach.

13

ABOUT "THE KNOCKED UP NUN
AND HER PECULIAR HEN"

~

First published: March 2023
      Tales of Fear, Superstition, and Doom

WHEN RELIGION MEETS SUPERSTITION, one nun's world is about to get very dark. Thank goodness she has a demon chicken.

14

THE KNOCKED UP NUN AND HER PECULIAR HEN

BY ANGELIQUE FAWNS

The crow that screamed in the ancient oak tree made it hard to focus on my morning prayers. His antics shook the branches and dropped leaves on the stone walkway in the convent's rose garden. Red blooms perfumed the air, even as they wilted in the midday July heat. In spite of the screeching of that black bird, I loved the serenity of this place. Life is easier when I can follow the rules and let God guide my actions. At least that's what I believed before I was seduced by a devil.

"I'm not interested in your dark omens, birdie," I said to the crow, clutching the gold band around my neck. It's damp from the sweat that had soaked through my heavy woolen habit. The ring is an unusual piece, handmade with embossed Celtic love knots. I never take it off.

A hand touches my shoulder. "Sister Helen, you must come immediately. Your father is sick," said Mother Superior.

"May the Lord hasten his healing. I pray I can return here soon." I wiped a tear from my eye then hurried to my room and packed my meager belongings into an old sack. I'd only just arrived for my semi-nary schooling and had a premonition the crow's message of bad luck was just beginning.

~

THE RUSTY TAXI shuddered and swerved on the dirt road as we pulled up to the tired farmhouse. I caught my breath. My father's prized vegetable garden was a mess of deer-chewed corn and rotten tomatoes. The scarecrow had collapsed into the dirt, his bright clothes moldy with mud. The fox gnawing on a rat gave us a dirty look for disturbing his dinner, then tucked tail and ran into the weedy field. When I gave the cabbie his fare, I saw his eyes were crusted with cataracts and dread grabbed my heart with icy fingers. Lunging out of the car, I ran up the sagging porch and into the neglected house.

"My lamb, you've returned. Keep up your prayers and studies here, okay?" Sean O'Malley hugged me; his arms quivering with the effort. "Your mom would have been mightily proud of you."

I filled him full of hot tea and chicken soup, and he made a shaky recovery. But he was nowhere near strong enough to take off the hay that needed to be harvested.

"The Lord will provide," I murmured, looking out the window at the tall alfalfa.

There was a man in stained orange overalls in the vegetable garden. He was bending over our fallen scarecrow.

I rushed out, not even taking the time to tidy my long hair or remove my flour-dusted apron.

"Can I help you?"

The man finished righting our scarecrow on its wooden spine before he gave me his attention. He was thin and hungry-looking. When he took off his ball cap, a torrent of dark curly hair fell to his shoulders. What really caught my attention were his two different colored eyes. One blue and one grey. I shuddered; it was like he was peering into my very soul.

"Eh, the farmer up the road said you might be needing help with the hay? I'm Henri, *bonjour*." He grinned as he set the ball cap at a jaunty angle on the scarecrow's head. "This cap brings me the good luck."

"Well, we can use help and good fortune." I smiled, charmed.

"I help out in the field for the food and a bed," he nodded. His French-Canadian accent made my heart flutter. His ghost eyes promising me a future.

Henri moved into our dusty guest room on the three-season porch, but he left his hat on the scarecrow.

Stacking the heavy hay bales was a thankless job, so I brought him a cool pitcher of ice tea in the mid-afternoon. The old rooster barred my way, flying up at my legs as I walked to the field. I had to run to evade his sharp beak, arriving with flushed cheeks and long strands of blonde hair loose from my bun.

"Now I know why Adam was tempted --you are my Eve, my Jezebel, tabernacle," Henri whispered into the back of my neck.

The chills traveling down my spine were delicious and I learned the true meaning of rolling in the hay. Henri ripped my ring off my neck in his brief passion, then rolled off me, and went right back to work. Trembling and sore, I searched the barn mumbling fervent prayers to St. Anthony, the saint of lost things. I found the ring, but my virginity was lost forever.

There was no blaming the crow for this; I'd broken my vow of chastity willingly. Sobbing, I realized I could never return to the convent, and soon I couldn't disguise the growing bump under my loosest flowered dress.

Sean O'Malley took his shotgun out to the bunkhouse by the old barn and cornered Henri. "I should shoot you, you French fecker, but you'll make an honest woman out of her, you will!"

We got married the next week in a no-frills ceremony. I took my mother's wedding ring off my neck and gave it to my husband to slide on my finger. We had a few pleasant days of dancing and playing at making house, but Henri had a short attention span. Soon our marriage was just Henri's occasional drunk visit to my bedroom, until the growing bump of my belly turned him off.

"Lord, you are fatter than the cows in the field," he growled, going off to drink beer in the shed.

With the rains of November, a chill settled on the old farm. My father's pneumonia returned, and no amount of chicken soup could save him. After Sean O'Malley died, Henri drank the hay harvest money, then sold off our few cows and pigs to buy more beer.

Instead of working the fields, Henri pummeled me with his fists. Though I'd tucked an acorn into my apron as a potent symbol of fertility and life, I gave birth to a stillborn son. Beautiful in his blue skin, I couldn't even cry for him.

"Too bad, a son would have been nice to help wid the fields. But who needs the extra mouth to feed, eh?" Henri said.

The future he was seeing with those heterochromia eyes was a life of ease for himself and hell for me.

I spent long hours sitting in the grass with the only livestock left. A few old chickens. Tears silently wetting my face. Angry at God, I spent less time praying and focused my attentions on feeding my old girls high-protein foods and good grains. All the crusts from toast. The fat off Henri's steak.

"I like to see you busy, woman. You go ahead and feed them chickens anything you want," he said.

The rooster that attacked me on the day of the hay harvest mounted the hens he'd been ignoring for years. In the old shed that doubled as a chicken coop, I finally saw a broody hen sitting on a pile of eggs that had hatched. I would have fresh chickens in five months! Seven of the chicks had downy red feathers, which meant they were females, and huddled together for warmth. The eighth chick, black with murky yellow eyes, sat apart from the group. She didn't even shiver, so still she could have been an evil Easter toy.

I picked her up to snap her wee neck, but when she squawked and flapped her wings in a fury, I put her in a nesting box and made sure she had enough grain and water. I admired her feistiness. Soon, the new girls were producing a good number of light brown eggs. My odd hen did lay, but her eggs came out black and shiny. A soft-shelled egg is bad luck and I always toss them immediately over the house. I contemplated tossing these ones, but they were the opposite of soft with a satisfying heft. Instead, I hid them in my father's tractor shed.

I put a cooler of eggs for sale at the end of the driveway and the money trickled in. Henri stopped his drunk visits to my bed and slowed down with the slaps. I assumed he had found a girlfriend in town. Even if he was committing the cardinal sin of infidelity, I was fine with that. I did not need to be cursed with another baby.

The hard work of housekeeping and laboring in my chicken coop made my fingers swell, so I would use butter at night to take my ring off. I always put it in the same place on my bedside table. One morning the ring wasn't there. Though I scoured my entire bedroom, I didn't find it.

"Henri, have you seen my ring?" I asked.

"Don't bother me with your absent-minded ways, woman, I'm reading the paper," Henri scratched his belly and turned a greasy page.

He was wearing his favorite ball cap again. When had he taken it off the scarecrow? Did he care so little for me and the farm that he wouldn't share even a smidgen of good luck?

I ran to the chicken coop, my refuge. When I opened the door to let my hens out, I saw chewed holes in my grain bags. Enormous rats scurried under the floorboards when the light interrupted their dinner.

"Saint Francis of Assisi, stop these dastardly creatures from stealing my profits," I said to the sky.

The patron saint of animals didn't answer, but my black hen squawked, spreading her wings like a cormorant. I carried her out to the grass to join the rest of the flock, picked up her daily black egg, and made my way down to my father's barn. The old building smelled like oil, fertilizer and cattle. While hiding my eggs in a corner, I saw small black boxes and green blocks labeled "Rodenticide" on a shelf above. That was how my father had dealt with vermin.

The next morning when I opened the splintery wood door, there was a disemboweled rat in the sawdust. My black hen was pecking at the eyes of another.

"That's a good start," I said to her, laying the black boxes with rat poison by the holes in the floor, "but this should be more effective."

Blood dripping from her beak, she let me shoo her away and I used a shovel to toss the rat carcasses into the ditch on the other side of the road.

I went back into the barn for a final sniff of nostalgia. Grief for my father and lost child overwhelmed me for a minute and I leaned on the old tractor parked by the swinging doors of the equipment storage area.

"The Lord helps those who help themselves." I summoned courage.

The tractor was an old green John Deere with peeling paint and a raccoon-chewed seat. I gathered my stained farm dress into one hand and climbed up. There was a key in the ignition caked with dirt. Taking a deep breath, I pushed the clutch and the brake while turning the key. The old beast rumbled to life and a sudden rush of blood made me light-headed. I was exhausted and trembling. The old Helen would never be so brave. Killing rats and climbing on tractors?! I turned it off, jumped down and went into the house for a cool glass of water.

Tap. Tap. Tap.

An odd knocking sound, like a small child hitting the door with a stick.

Tap. Tap. Tap.

Opening the door, I heard a cooing. My black hen. Blood was splattered across her chest and dripping from her beak.

"Are you hurt?"

She hopped down the porch, then screeched.

"You seem fine. Whose blood is that, birdie?"

She hopped a few more steps, looked back at me, then ran, flapping her wings across the lawn. I followed her back to the chicken coop. The rooster was dead, half-eaten. A fox stood over him; one eye bloodied from a peck.

"Damn fox! You were eating the rats, and when I killed them, you decided to upgrade to chickens? Get out of here?" I flapped my hands.

The fox didn't move. He wasn't giving up his chicken dinner. The rest of my birds were huddled in the corner, heads down, wings flat.

Most chickens freeze when terrified but my black hen flew up and squawked at the creature, snapping her sharp beak. The fox snarled at her. I grabbed the shovel outside the door and whacked the creature on the head. The fox slumped to the ground, tongue protruding.

"I don't know if you would have won that fight, birdie," I said to my black hen, giving my flock some fresh grain.

I said a few words of prayer over the dead fox and then dragged the predator to the burn pile.

When Henri came home that night, I was excited.

"You won't believe what happened today—" I clapped my hands.

He interrupted, "Vera is coming to live with us next week. She'll be taking your bed and you can move out into the guest room."

"Is Vera your girlfriend? How can you even consider that? Under the eyes of God, we are married and I will not have you living in sin under my own roof."

Henri shut my mouth with his fists and I cringed with every hard slap. I saw his handsome face wrinkle with rage as his hand hit my temple. I don't know if that was the end of the beating, but blissfully for me, it was the end of my memory of it.

I assume he carried me to the guest room because the next morning I woke up sweaty and sore on the couch. I gingerly tested out my limbs. Nothing broken, just bruised and banged up. An intense headache pounded at my temples but I took up my rosary to say prayers in spite of the pain. The throbbing defeated my piousness so I only managed half the beads before I cast it aside.

I stumbled into the kitchen, counting my blessings that Henri must have left already for town. His cap sat on the kitchen table, the dirty thing right where I would like to eat my breakfast. Ignoring the rumbling in my belly, I snatched it up. Toast would have to wait and I limped out to the garden to put the hat back on the scarecrow.

Frowning, I regarded it. I doubted the hat had much power, but who was I to challenge superstition?

Protecting my sore side, I hobbled to the coop and let the chickens into the grass. My black hen jumped into my arms, cooing and rubbing her head on my black eye.

"Now go on there, girl, Henri isn't a rat or a fox. You can't help me with this," I gently tossed her after the flock eating worms in the grass.

Gathering the eggs, I put the brown ones aside while tucking the shiny black egg into my apron and walking to the barn. My growing collection of black orbs gleamed in an impressive pile hidden under the corner shelf. I knew mice wouldn't be interested in the inedible eggs and Henri was too lazy to leave his armchair. I drew in a deep breath of oily air and walked over to the John Deere.

"Good Lord, give me strength to try again!"

I climbed up onto the tractor and started the engine. This time I put my foot on the gas and lurched a few feet forward. Finding the right balance between the clutch and the accelerator, I drove around the barnyard. My black hen watched me from a fence post, clucking and flapping her wings with joy. Every jostle hurt, but I reveled in the pain. Freedom. The smell of diesel burned my nostrils as I turned down the driveway. A smile pulled at my lips until I was distracted by another crow in the front yard tree.

Then disaster.

One of the tires slipped off the driveway into the drainage ditch and the tractor jolted to a stop at a precarious angle. My blood ran cold.

"He gives strength to the weary and increases the power of the weak," I said to my black hen as she gnashed her beak and jumped into the weeds.

The grumble of the old pickup truck coming down the driveway meant Henri was home early. He parked by the ditched tractor and I clambered off quickly. A young woman jumped out of the passenger side. This must be Vera. She looked no older than twenty and had dark curls pulled into a ponytail. Her eyes had the dull look of one whose mental capacity was far less than her years. She grabbed Henri's hand and I noticed the distinctive Celtic love knot design of my mother's ring on her finger.

"My ring! Henri you thieving devil."

"Forget the ring, Helen. Tabernacle, what did you do to the tractor?"

He lunged and grabbed my hair, dragging me to the house. Vera followed making mewling sounds of fear and confusion. The first slaps were slow and measured. My rage at the theft of my mother's ring was so great, I hardly felt them.

Tap. Tap. Tap.

Henri paused his beating. "What's that?"

Vera was hunched against the wall.

Tap. Tap. Tap.

"Sounds like someone is at the door. You better get it," I mumbled through a split lip.

Tap. Tap. Tap.

He stalked over the cracked cement floor to the front door.

I licked my bleeding lip. "Henri be quick. 'It is mine to avenge; I will repay. In due time their foot will slip; their day of disaster is near and their doom rushes upon them' I haven't forgotten all of my seminary schooling you adulterer."

He opened the screen door and looked around in confusion.

"There's no one ... ahhh!"

My black hen flew up at his face and pecked at his blue eye. His grey one was swollen and closed. Henri stumbled backward. Wings flapping, pecking ferociously, Henri and Vera's screams combining into a cacophony of horror.

"What in damnation, *merde,* " he fell to the ground, his hands covering his bleeding face.

Henri's meaty fists flew as he tried to fight off the rampaging bird.

"Don't you hurt my chicken," I kicked at his knees, knocking him to the ground

My hen pecked his throat and Vera's screaming reached a new pitch. If the black bird hit his artery, Henri might actually die. Still kicking at his legs, I felt adrenaline energize my body. This must be blood lust. My hen and I were powerful. I was powerful. We were going to kill the devil. I kicked even harder. His remaining blue eye met mine. Hyperventilating, I fought the urge to kick and kick and kick. He wasn't worth it.

"My Patron Saint of Livestock, we are not going to commit the soul-destroying sin of murder," I said, scooping the black hen off Henri and putting her on my shoulder.

Henri rolled onto his stomach, groaning, a little bit of blood seeping from his neck to the floor.

"You and your new concubine will leave my land. I will never hear from you again," my hen punctuated my command with a deep cluck.

Henri slowly pulled himself to his feet, one hand at his bloody throat. Vera rushed over and grabbed his arm.

"Vera, that is my mother's ring and I will have it back," I said, a bit more gently.

Trembling, she pulled my ring off her finger and I put my hen on the ground to take it. I slipped it back where it belonged.

"Go!"

"This is my farm, you vicious bitch." Henri said.

"Wrong. I inherited this farm. It's mine."

My hen stretched her wings, cawing a warning.

"You are cursed, *mon Dieu*, you and that damned animal of yours!" Henri said.

He leaned on Vera and stumbled a few steps, "Can I at least get my lucky ball cap?" He pointed one trembling hand at the scarecrow in the front field.

"You silly, superstitious man. There is no future for you here. Take your ghost eyes and leave." I lifted my chin.

His shoulders sagged and Vera sobbed into her palms. They climbed into the truck and I watched them drive away. If he dares to return, my father has some old hunting rifles in the barn. I will teach myself how to use them.

"The meek shall inherit the earth!" I put my hands on my hips and looked around the farm. My land. With no Henri and his evil soul to darken it.

If I'd managed to survive off a few egg sales, imagine what I could do with the entire farm? The tractor and all the tools were here. I could get to know people now that Henri wasn't around to run them off. There were many challenges ahead. My stomach churned, but this time in excitement.

I thought about my hidden store of shiny black eggs in the barn. Could they be a precious type of material? Carbonado, tourmaline or onyx? If they had worth, the farm could be a refuge for fallen women. A place to study the Bible and live peacefully. Where one blunder (like sleeping with the farm help) doesn't have to ruin your whole life. If God forgives, why couldn't the convent allow for a few broken vows? There would be room for mistakes here.

My black hen made her way to the front garden to join the other birds pecking bugs off the vines. I looked at the scarecrow still wearing Henri's sweaty ball cap. I knocked it off and ground it into the dirt with my heel. There was no good luck in that hat. The best thing that ever happened to me was a peculiar black hen. The Lord does work in mysterious ways.

Taking a deep breath, I let the serenity and peace of the afternoon wash over me. My nose twitched with the smell of ripening tomatoes. A crow landed on the scarecrow where Henri's hat once sat. I smiled at it. Black birds bring me luck. The crow bobbed his head in greeting and flew up into the reddening sky, the raucous caw promising me many wonderful days to come.

15

ABOUT "FORGET-ME-NOT AND MORNING DEW"

First published: January 2023
Murderbirds: An Avian Anthology

YELENA CRANE IS a guest author in this collection, and she joins this anthology with a tale about feathers, the human spirit, and a birdbrain.

WITH AN ADVANCED DEGREE in the sciences, Yelena has followed her passions from mad scientist to sci-fi/spec writer. Her stories often explore the complexities of human nature, and the consequences of our choices. She's published in Nature Futures, DSF, Dark Matter Ink, Flame Tree, and elsewhere. Follow her on twitter @Aelintari and https://www.yelenacrane.com/.

16

FORGET-ME-NOT AND MORNING DEW

BY YELENA CRANE

*I*gnore my slicked-down feather-mane, my stilt-legs that kick with power five times my weight, my wings that rip through air—I am a man. I will be man again.

A spell gone wrong, and now my sentience wastes beneath plumage, scorching in the savanna sun.

Blackest Crest and Longest Lashes strut ahead of me on their fine legs. Those aren't the secretary birds' real names. What's in a name when the air is rank with pheromones? When I try to mimic them, my own footing is unsure. I've never had legs so thin and hollow before. Two days less human, and I'm still all kook.

There's a strong impulse to hunt hunt hunt and eat eat eat I must ignore. The more I let the raptor instincts take over, the more I lose myself. There are four things I must remember above all else: bush-willow branches, forget-me-nots, fresh morning dew, and the magic words.

A pattern of vibrations tells me the others were successful in flushing out food. From their stomps, I can tell the prey is small and slippery. A snake. The emptiness in my stomach pulsates. A reminder I want that meat. I want everything that moves within stomping distance. My gullet has no discrimination against bug, reptile, or

75

rodent; it wants only to be fed. It repulses me, the things I've eaten and enjoyed.

"Wait for me!" The bushwillow branches I'd been gathering fall with a thunk. "I'm coming just now!" I don't know if my thoughts translate proper into bird-talk because the others only speak to me through the hammer of their feet on the cracking clay.

It's kief how the world becomes sepia from my kicked-up dust when I run all knobby-ankled to catch up. They greet me with nature's music of beak-ripped flesh.

"Eish, leave some for me!" The puff adder is colors I've no words for and couldn't see before with human eyes. Colors as delicious as the meat.

Blackest Crest has the snake's head, plus some, hanging from her beak. She'd have swallowed it entire except Longest Lashes is at the other end. The snake's tail still has some whip of life in it.

Food strengthens the contractions in my gut until it's all I can think of. Calculations whir in my birdbrain that I don't quite under-stand—a notion I'd been busy before with something important.

The fussing over who gobbles down more of the hisser distracts me yet again. Reminds me I won't likely see any morsel of that sweet flesh. All that energy running here, wasted.

A snake that big means rodents nearby. The landscape is flat as far as the eye can see, and my new eyes see far. The sound is soft when I hear it, wind brushing against stalks except there is no wind.

Prey.

I fight the impulse. There's bushwillows in the distance I need to get to. My wings pump and I'm airborne. Flying toward them feels like flying toward my humanity. From this distance, the view is almost worth it. The horizon's near bare except for buttons of acacia trees scattered over clumps of dirt. Scarves of waterholes peek from the dust.

A kite's up ahead on the hunt. I know I can get what it's chasing faster on the ground. I land, ready to trample, forgetting why I ever made so much effort to fly.

The kite, who'd been here first, don't welcome my presence.

"Yoh!" The arrogance of birds still shocks me. "It didn't have your name on it," I say. If he don't like the competition, he's in the wrong field of work. "How about we make a jol of it?"

There's a prattle on the ground only scampering food—that don't know it's food—makes. It'll have to do for club music. My wings dance, flashing open and closed so fast the lizard and kite don't know where to focus.

Stomp go my feet, before my mind can think it.

The kite's all wings again, trying to outmaneuver me from the heavens. Failing. Shame for the old bru, running on South Africa late-time means leaving on an empty stomach, because the lizard's already caught between my stocky toes. The kite won't get mercy from me. It flies off, chirping insults and skindering untruths about me to the clouds.

The meat's warm and raw as air when I swallow it whole, warm still when I cough up a pellet of bones. Lizard's not man food, I think, looking down at the forbidden sausage. There are three things I must remember above all else: bushwillows, morning dew, and words.

I'm all mouth, gathering branches and grass when Blackest Crest swoops down close. "Can you understand me? Can you help?" I ask.

She angles her head left, angles it right. Silent except for the ruffle of her feathers.

"Where's Long Lashes then?" I ask.

No answer.

Better I don't know, that I don't entangle myself in the lives of these birds. Better except there's her scent again and a newer instinct taking hold of me, a whisper, for now, saying mate mate mate. I don't remember a woman ever being so irresistible as she, a crest so iridescent.

Now is not the time for such thoughts. I've paid for each hour as a secretary bird with memories of who I used to be. Hours I spent collecting ingredients. I'm running out of time if I let distraction delay me.

There are two things I need: bushwillow branches and the magic words.

~

MY PILE IS ALMOST READY, wide enough to bed a human body since I don't know if the spell will also transport me back to my flat in Johannesburg or change me here. I'm willing to take the risk. Man has survived worse than savanna with secretary birds. I'm searching for one last branch when there's an unexpected shadow overhead. It's Long Lashes, giving chase. I don't realize what toward, until it's too late and he's landed on my day's work.

"Stop!"

He's kicking faster than I can run. By the time I'm close enough to shoo him off, the long, elegant branches I walked kilometers to find are broken and scattered chips. Long Lashes don't even notice me.

"Why?" My nictitating membrane swallows up my tears so I can't even get a good cry. It makes me more furious. I follow after Long Lashes to force an answer out of him even though the only answer can be he thought there was food inside.

His feather tail is a beak's reach away and I take the bite. "Ears clogged? Yebo or no?"

Long Lashes croaks hoarsely, stomping his feet backward at me. I don't know what it is we're doing, until we're flapping wings and take the fight skyward. I kick him for destroying my hard work. Kick because I fear the pile wouldn't have turned me back anyway. Or worse, the man-me was never real and I'm a secretary bird born, raised, and gone crazy. All the frustration and anger works down into my legs. Into my beak when I croak in rapid bursts, not saying anything, just making noise.

I don't know what I've done or how tired I am until Long Lashes plunges down from one thousand meters and it's all my fault. I've murdered my own kind—no, not my own.

I'm human, damnit.

It's easy to trace Long Lashes. When I find him, he's in a bed of short grass and looks nothing like himself. He's two crooked legs, a bloodied chest, and a bashed-in human skull. "Long Lashes?" It's him, I can smell it from a kilometer away. I'm poking softly at him.

"Please be alive. I'm sorry, so sorry." He doesn't move. I'm a murderer in truth now, a killer of my own kind; of two. I take in his human form again and wonder if any birds are real or man's fantasy for flight.

Standing over Long Lashes's corpse, I pray for forgiveness, though I'd never been a praying man. I pray death's not the only way to reverse the spell. There's no way to even get Long Lashes proper buried, my talons aren't built for scooping up clay or rocks.

Bushwillow branches and special words, I must not forget. Will secretary bird croaks do? They must. For me and for Long Lashes.

IT'S JUST AFTER ALL the morning dew is dried and instead of hunting, I'm spitballing rhymes that do nothing but make me hungry. Blackest Crest takes to the skies and offers pleasant shade when she blots the sun. For the first time since we've met, she's undulating and croaking. Without meaning to, my wings flap up and I join her. Midair, our talons clasp. The air's thick with her perfume and the music of our wings flapping in courtship. "Were you human once too?"

I'm forgetting one important thing, words.

I remember! The words find me in the sky with Blackest Crest, interspersed with the strong impulse to mate mate mate. "O beautifulest of birds, beautifulest of creatures. Notice my slicked down feather-mane. My stilt-legs. My wings. Pick me."

17

ABOUT "FARMYARD FOLLILES"

~

First published: December 2020
The Story Behind the Stories

LAYING hens have a short commercial life span for egg production. But these birds have a great clucking plan, PLUS some magic talents.

18

FARMYARD FOLLIES

BY ANGELIQUE FAWNS

Farmer Martin Ross sips his coffee but finds the flavour bitter. His brew always starts to taste nasty right around county fair time. Could envy affect your taste buds? Running a hand over his shaved grey head he tries not to think of his arch nemesis. He has a rivalry with his next door neighbour. Goose Creek is only a small steamy town in the Carolina Lowcountry, but they take their local fairs seriously. Joel Miller raises pygmy goats and trains a team of them to do a routine while he blows cues on a trumpet. While his long beard swings and his cowboy boots tap, the goats jump around in different formations and then end the act with a big pyramid, cute piled on top of cuter. Nobody can resist the four-legged cheerleaders, and Miller wins the talent contest at the local fair every year.

Ross runs a free-range chicken farm, and they sell the best eggs in the area. Happy chickens who get exposure to sunlight and lead a stress-free life produce eggs with thick yellow yolks, hard brown shells, and packed with Omega 3's. He has a Bantam rooster trained to run in circles around him, like a horse being lunged. It always gets a few laughs at the fair, but never the big win. He needs to find a chicken act that will leave Miller's drill team of nannies in the dust. With a sigh, Ross puts down his undrunk coffee and shrugs on his overalls. They hang loose on his thin frame, pounds lost to fair fretting. It's time to start his daily check-up of the fences and amount of grain in the silos. A new batch of laying hens came this morning and he wants to make sure everything is in good working order before he inspects them.

Meanwhile, it's chaos in the free-run chicken barn. The new arrivals are squawking and running amuck as they try to orient themselves. It may sound like just noise to the human ear, but the birds do have their own language.

"Where the cluck are we?" one girl shrieks.

"Get me the cluck out of here," another howls.

"That's my head you're standing on," comes from another.

Before today, they'd lived quietly in a small barn with only a few other chicks to avoid being squashed. Baby chicks are notorious for trampling each other. Talk about a life shock for them now. The large cover-all barn was almost wall-to-wall with hens and the noise deafening as new chickens collided with old birds. Dust shimmers in the sunlight as toes kick up sawdust and dried manure, making some of the old-timers cough and gag.

"Attention! All newcomers line up here. And we're not ducks, so no waddling! Get to it," a large black hen squawks above the ruckus.

Her voice thunders through the open space and everyone settles down. A group of four hens who'd been in the same shipping crate huddle together. They whisper among themselves, while the boss hen rounds up the more panicked stragglers.

"So what do sisters call yourselves? I'm Florence," a Red Sex-link bird says. She has lovely brown feathers and soft black eyes.

"I go by Mary," a cute Barred-Plymouth Rock says, "All four of us come from the same hatchery, but we can't be sisters being four different breeds," she puffs up her black and white foliage.

"Maybe we can be sisters by choice! Betty at your service here," a Columbian Rock with fine white feathers and mischievous grin joins in.

"Diana is my name," a Rhode Island Red says her eyes bright, not missing a thing, "this place is terrifying! I've never seen so many chickens in my life. What are there? Two hundred in here?"

Diana is interrupted by the boss hen hopping up on a large metal structure with multiple small boxes under it. Straw sticks out of each container, the odd egg, both brown and white, visible in some. She squawks for their attention.

"Welcome to the Ross Chicken Farm. I am the manager-on-the-floor and you can call me Barbara! You are all very lucky to live here. Most hens spend their lives in battery cages, but you are allowed to roam free and can even go outside for dust baths and sun bathing.

The four new friends look at each other in confusion. What is a battery cage?

"But there are rules here! You must lay your eggs in the laying berths. Do you see these little boxes I am standing on? You lay in here. Nowhere else. I catch you laying under the berths or in a corner, you will become soup!"

"Cluck me, Soup?" Florence says softly to Mary, "I guess that's a threat".

"Like we will have to make soup instead of eggs?" Betty asks.

"No," Mary says, "I think she means we will be the soup."

"That's ghastly!" Diana gasps.

"Silence, you cluckers!" she screams at the loud gaggle of four girls.

All the chickens freeze. A quiet settles over the barn with only the sound of the hanging feed dispensers creaking in the breeze.

"You will all lay at least one egg a day! No slackers here. If you stop laying, you will become soup," Barbara continues, "there is also a strict no fighting rule. No eye pecking, no feather pulling or else.... Soup!"

"Someone, somewhere, is eating a lot of soup." Betty whispers.

Barbara hops off the boxes and caws, "Follow me!"

All the new hens shuffle behind the large black bird as she starts pointing out the facilities. There are red waterers hanging from the ceiling on one side, while metal feeders hang down the other. The walls are taken up by the laying berths with big windows above them and the eggs roll down a ramp to an area under the barn. The most interesting part of the tour is the recreation area. There's a wall full of hay in a wired container for the girls to peck at, and kid's xylophones nailed to the wall. A few hens are bonking the different coloured keys with their beaks and random notes ring out.

"How long are we going to live here?" Mary asks, her cute puffy face creased in curiosity.

Barbara turns her dull body, the sheen of youth no longer on her feathers, and looks at the newbies, "The average stay is about a year, and when your egg production slacks off then it's time for..."

"Let me guess," Florence interrupts. "Soup!"

Some loud clucking, dust clouds, and random raining of feathers at one end of the barn distracts Barbara. It looks like too many chickens are trying to use the small door that leads to the outside pasture at the same time. As Barbara flaps off to check on the logjam, the girls look at one another.

"Well, I'm not sure how long a year is, but it doesn't sound long enough. What are we going to do when we stop laying eggs? Barbara is obviously older, what's her secret?" Betty frets.

Mary is distracted by the metal wiring on the hay dispenser and starts running her beak up and down it. She changes the rhythm and notes by strumming different length wires.

There is a reason these four chickens gravitated to one another. There is something special about all four of them. Not your average fowl.

Betty listens to the sound her friend is making, her white head cocked to one side as she nods to the beat. Then she starts flapping her wings right beside a metal feed container. As the strong bones hit the side of the metal, a low cool booming sound erupts.

Diana ruffles her red feathers in excitement and hops up to a xylophone. She pecks at the colored keys. Three short notes, three long ones. Something magical is happening to these impromptu instruments. The three girls manage to get their sounds in sync.

Florence hops up to another section of the hay wire and starts plucking with a toe, her harmony working perfectly with the others.

"I've been thinking about Barbara. I don't know how she avoids the soup pot, but I know one thing for sure," Florence opens her beak wide and goes from talking to singing, "there's no stopping us now. Now that we've found our way."

This has never happened before in this chicken barn. This has never happened before in any chicken barn anywhere else in the world. Florence, Mary, Betty, and Diana are pecking, singing, wing pounding and toe strumming like birds possessed. There is a joy and radiance around them that ushers in a new feeling of energy and possibility in the dusty barn. Every other chicken is silent and staring, beaks wide open, their red combs swaying to the beat. It is musical alchemy.

It's the four girl's luck that Farmer Ross walks in at that moment to check out his new flock. He drops his jaw in amazement listening to the catchy tune coming from the four different colored birds in the entertainment area. Then a slow smile crosses his face. An evil, delicious, delighted smile. Wait till Joel Miller sees what he is bringing to the local fair. Wait till everyone sees and hears! He is going to win the talent show for sure this year. In fact, he's pretty sure the local fair is only the beginning. These are some special birds. Time to pour a fresh cup of coffee, and Ross knows it will taste great.

19

ABOUT "THE HEALING BREATH OF ALPACAS"

*A*n Original Story for Peculiar Pets

BRANDON CASE IS a guest author in this collection, and a story about alien alpacas? Yes, please.

BRANDON CASE IS an erstwhile government cog who fled the doldrums into unsettling worlds of science and magic. He has recent work in Escape Pod, Air and Nothingness Press, and The Dread Machine, among others. You can catch his alpine adventures on Twitter and Instagram @BrandonCase101.

20

THE HEALING BREATH OF ALPACAS

BY BRANDON CASE

Karen stumbled out of the US Army helicopter in Washington DC, her cotton sundress snapping like a paisley flag. She balanced her two-year-old son on one hip, staring out at the sea of people gathered beneath a monstrous, purple spaceship the size of Cleveland.

Seeing online images of the alien ships had been unsettling... but nothing could've captured their domineering size. Like what a baby must feel, looking up at their parent. Were they here to punish humanity? And why on earth had *she* been summoned?

Army soldiers forced open a path through the throng. Following them, Karen approached a raised stage. A Secret Service agent in dark glasses leaned close and said, "The president and her advisors will feed you answers. Say only what they tell you. God knows why the alien wanted a midwestern housewife to speak for the entire United States—but they requested you by social security number."

The agent took Karen's son away and ushered her onto the dais. At its center stood an alpaca the size of a tank. A cloud of purple particles draped its fluffy shoulders like judicial robes. On a podium next to the animal sat a transparent cube the size of Karen's head. It displayed video feeds showing alpacas speaking with citizens of other countries.

The aliens are... alpacas?

The president of the United States stood off to one side of the stage. In a deathly serious tone, she said, "Karen, it's incredibly important that you—"

The alpaca-alien made a curt gesture with its foreleg; a blue dome solidified around Karen and the creature, reducing the outside world to a veil of crackling static. Tendrils of ozone drifted off the barrier, the tangy scent of lightning.

"Good," the alpaca-alien said in a stately voice. "We can begin."

"What do you want from me?"

"Consider us galactic law enforcement. Your species is on trial. We asked for a quintessentially average member of your country to serve as its representative. That's you."

Karen patted her shoulder-length brown hair. "Am I really that average?"

"Quite. Now, are you aware of the damage incurred to this planet's ecosystem in the last century?"

"I think so. No more rainforests. The poor polar bears all died."

"And are you aware of the role humanity played in this destruction?"

Outside, fists thumped against the blue barrier. Muffled shouts.

"Uh..." Karen said. "Everyone knows about climate change. But I recycle, and at my house we have Vegan-Thursdays."

"A serviceable admission of guilt. Now, while we can't force your species to change, would you like to restore the environment yourselves?"

"Of course! But—"

"Contract established." The alpaca-alien turned to the transparent cube, and its toe tapped icons with a rapid staccato rivaling a teenager's texting thumbs. "My fellow judges all concur. That concludes this trial."

"Wait, what do you mean trial?" Karen's hand leaped to her chest, trying to cover a hollowed-out feeling. Had she made things worse? "What's going to happen?"

"Remediation. Nothing too onerous—galactic law prohibits us from murder or the outright destruction of your culture. You'll lose those pesky opposable thumbs for a few generations. We're also rewiring your body to consume carbon dioxide and emit oxygen... that way you'll be restoring the climate with your own lungs."

"Rewiring?" She did *not* like the sound of that.

"Yes. You'll wear the shape of your planet's most morally elevated creature to serve as an example. The same one we adopted today to put you at ease."

Wait... did that mean—

Karen gasped as the blue shell shattered.

Outside, pandemonium erupted. Purple particles rained from the spaceship. Twisting, luminous sparkles that flitted through the air like flocks of starlings. As the colorful cloud overtook the crowd, fleeing people froze in place.

Karen dove for her son. Inches away, she jerked to a stop with her arms outstretched. The air around her solidified, hard as stone. Her heart hammered. Numb tingles replaced all feeling in Karen's body. Her mind fell quiet; stifled calm, like a hooded bird.

The crowd's screams drifted into silence. Purple hoops formed around everyone like the ovals used to draw animal figures. Scaffolding, refined to four-legged outlines. Human bodies unraveled into strips of skin, muscle, and nerve that wound over the guiding forms. Flesh grew to fill the gaps. New skin sprouted ubiquitous, springy hair.

Just like that, every human in the crowd had transformed into an alpaca.

The galactic judge patted the President of the United States on her fluffy, gray head. Then, in a swirl of purple robes, the alien soared up to its spaceship.

"Mom?" a baby alpaca cried, inches from Karen's outstretched forelegs. The little animal looked up at her with big, brown eyes.

Karen sucked in a breath of air that tasted like carbonated water.

Kneeling, she cradled her son between her furry legs, repeating, "It's okay, it's okay."

"You!" The alpaca-president pointed her forefoot at Karen. "What the hell did you say to it? Take her into custody!"

Karen stepped in front of her son, who peeked around her bushy leg. Somehow, her sundress had survived the transformation; she smoothed it with her fetlock and said, "I told the truth."

"Madam President?" The alpaca-agent with dark sunglasses stood on his hind legs, fumbling with his handcuffs; they slipped through his forefeet and dropped to the stage.

The alpaca-president sighed. "I suppose our agents will need to carry bridles, now…"

Above them, the purple spaceship rose out of the atmosphere, vanishing with a *crack* that echoed among the herd of erstwhile humans.

"Tell me everything that transpired," the alpaca-president said.

Karen carefully repeated the exchange.

The alpaca-president listened—interrupting now and then to issue orders for securing hay supplies and organizing an evacuation into the grasslands. Finally, she said, "I don't think you understand the consequences of your negligent actions."

"You're blaming *me* for this?" Karen spat on the stage. "I guess we're still human, no matter our shape."

Her son nuzzled her with his fluffy head.

Karen hummed softly to him, and said, "At least the planet gets to rest while we're in time-out."

21

ABOUT "INVASIVE SPECIES"

~

First published: January 2021
DreamForge

Is it possible aliens already live among us? What if those aliens are psychic bugs?

22

INVASIVE SPECIES

BY ANGELIQUE FAWNS

A YEAR AGO

Brad Smudge rested a hand on his daughter's shoulder as they surveyed the rows of cannabis plants. The smell of ripe buds hung heavy in the greenhouse and some of the green leaves were turning yellow. Moisture dripped off the glass and sweat trickled down Cass's skin under her tank top.

The old farmer took a deep breath, "darlin, that there's the smell of money."

"It smells like skunk. Would this stuff survive outside?"

She raised her voice over the sound of rain pattering down on the glass roof. It was the end of August and thunder-stormed almost every day. Very atypical weather for the Greater Toronto Area.

"Mary Jane likes it warm with just the perfect bit of humidity, she doesn't like to get her knickers damp. This dang summer's been wetter than an otter's pocket."

Cass strolled down the rows of plants, the heads on them dark and turning a reddish color. Her father followed with a notepad, taking a final count of his inventory.

The greenhouse was the size of a large backyard pool and it took a second mortgage on the farm to build it. It had been nearly invisible at the rear of the property, until her dad had installed his LED grow lights. He'd put them in a couple weeks ago, complaining bitterly about the added cost and how, "the cussin' clouds were stoppin' the sun from doing its damn job."

The farm was very private, being surrounded by several hectares of crown land. But now Brad Smudge's Grow Op could be seen glowing at night. He'd hooked up a gas generator to power the lights and was bringing in fuel by the gallons.

If her mother was alive, she would have shut old Brad Smudge's pot emporium down in a New York minute. Arlene Smudge had been a ferocious Métis woman and her French-Canadian spice, tempered with the farming wisdom from her indigenous heritage, kept the family firmly grounded. But now there was no one to harness Brad's wild ideas and he was making some risky decisions.

"Didn't Carl from across the road come tell you it was dangerous to grow this stuff? Wasn't a Grow Op a few concessions over robbed?"

"Carl should mind his own damn business. Who takes advice from a guy trying to farm Buffalo meat? Just because he drives around on that rusty Harley Davidson, he thinks he's some kind of criminal know-it-all."

"I hear Buffalo is a great low-fat alternative, but Dad, back to what you're trying to farm. Are you sure this is a legal grow? You're not great at paperwork."

"I already have a buyer for it. The Alcohol and Gaming Commission believe it or not. They are sending their inspector tomorrow and then it's steak dinner for us!"

Her father was short and muscular with just a slight beer belly. His thick hair stuck out like a hockey player under his John Deere ball cap. Cass inherited his body shape, minus the stomach pot, with her own spectacular spill of long dark hair. Her light brown skin and sensible nature came from her mother. A sudden wave of love washed over her watching him tend his crop. After Arlette died of cancer last year, they'd learned to depend on each other, becoming very close. Her mom had used hash oil in her tea for nausea relief near the end.

"Look at these darn bugs," he said, pulling a shiny green beetle out of the soil.

The bug crawled over his hand, trying to scuttle back to its dark spot, and Brad shuddered, "Dang gone it, got me a bad feeling about these things. Your ma was the one for premonitions, but I think I'm havin' one."

He tried to squash the bug between two thick callused fingers, but it shot out of his hand unharmed and disappeared into the dirt.

"Can they ruin your sale?" Cass asked.

"Not if I have anything to do with it. I'll scour each and every plant. Even if it takes till sun rise."

"It's already getting past seven Dad; you should get your rest."

"Nope. A farmer tends to his crop. Now throw your rain jacket on and head out."

Cass stepped into the deluge and ran towards the house. The corn plants on the rest of their acreage wilted under the rain, the stalks small from too much moisture. They wouldn't even be able to harvest it this fall if the land didn't dry up.

She hoped she'd get a good night's sleep. It was a big day for her tomorrow. She was starting her internship at a local media company in Toronto, part of her film college program. Steven Spielberg -move over.

Cass banged through the screen door, peeling off her wet clothes and littering the hall. The decor of the farmhouse was simple and comfortable. She walked along the frayed carpet to the bathroom and drew herself a bath in the clawfoot tub. Pouring in some of her favorite bubble bath, she drifted off in the warm suds. Her eyes flew open when she heard what sounded like a gun.

She sat up quickly in the bath water, now cold. Who shot skeet at night? And hunting season wasn't for months. She threw on a bathrobe, grabbed her cell phone, and charged out the door in her rubber boots. The trail was muddy; the sky black with clouds; the rain a light drizzle.

She stopped when she saw the headlights of several ATV's with tow-behind trailers parked outside the greenhouse. Piles of plants were tossed haphazardly in the dump carts. Four dark forms moved among them. Her throat spasmed and Cass threw a hand up to her mouth to stop from calling out. Tucking herself behind one of the larger trees, she pulled her cell phone out of her pocket. A tear slid down her face, she couldn't risk calling for help right now and draw attention to herself. She waited until she heard the ATV's driving off through the bush towards the crown land.

When she was sure they were gone, she dialed 911 while slipping and scrambling through the mud to the greenhouse.

"Dad, are you okay," she wrenched open the door with slippery hands.

Her dad was tied to a chair. Blood matting his thick dark hair where two bullets had torn through his head.

PRESENT DAY

The shiny green beetle crawled off the backpack and onto the wide white desk. Multiple legs propelling it towards Cass's arm. Tentacles twice the size of its inch-long body gently probed her hand resting on the mouse. Her eyes teared as a vision of her father, though he was distorted and enormous, filled her mind. The image changed to a swarm of green bugs on a dune-filled landscape, scuttling over dead bent trees. Cass blinked, feeling a tickle on her right hand. One of those horrid bugs was on her pinky finger. She remembered her father finding a beetle the day he died. His killers hadn't been caught and she phoned the police once a week looking for updates. She hadn't had a good night sleep since the murder, trying to figure out why someone would kill her father over some stupid plants.

Now one had hitched its way in with her to work. She grabbed a Kleenex and tried to crush it. Even though she gave it a good thump, it scurried away into the shadowy wires behind her monitor. She'd tell her boyfriend, an arborist specializing in invasive species, about the beetle later. Right now, she had a deadline to meet. Writing headlines for an agricultural website had to be done quickly to keep the "click rate" high. The more intriguing her line, the more people would click through to the full story, the more her company could charge advertisers.

Killer tomato blight creates huge market shortages

Cass tapped on her keyboard. She tugged on a strand of her black hair hard enough to hurt and hit delete.

Tomatoes die and farmers cry

Nope.

Fries without ketchup? Say it isn't so!

This line of copy would have to do.

The full news article talked about local restaurants forced to adjust their menus with a restricted supply of tomatoes. Not exactly the film career she'd hoped for, but she was lucky to have this job. When she lost her dad, she got enough in life insurance to pay off the debt on the farm, but not enough to keep herself in college.

Though devastated by his murder, she'd forced herself to drive to her internship the next day. And a good thing she did. When the marketing writer for the Farm News website went on maternity leave, Cass was in the right place at the right time. With global food insecurity becoming a thing, subscriber numbers were through the roof. Everyone wanted to know why grocery prices were so high. Most of her stories were about crop failures and infestations. The pictures were stomach churning. Black fruit, vegetables covered with fuzz, lots of those weird green bugs crawling everywhere in gloomy, rainy weather.

Heads sprout every twenty feet or so in the open concept plan at the office. It's the human equivalent of an industrial chicken farm. Big TV screens broadcast the different channels originating from the building. She'd love to move from website writing to TV Production. One step closer to her film dreams.

A news report on the TV closest to her was broadcasting about the unusually rainy weather. More than a year of above average precipitation. The Toronto Islands were almost completely submerged and everyone who lived there evacuated to the main land. The screen showed people canoeing down the bicycle paths with pets and carting bags of belongings. The show segued into a breaking news alert about crowds protesting the price of bread outside the Parliament buildings. Wheat crops suffered as much as corn this season.

Her work was on the shores of Lake Ontario, directly across from the Islands, and beside the Redpath Sugar factory. She had a good view of it from her desk. It was a huge brick building, with no windows and warehouse doors large enough for a transport truck. Water lapped at the concrete border, flooding the sidewalk with every wind surge. Sugar workers toiled diligently with sand bags to create a barrier.

She finished up the last headline and then packed her bag to go. Living on a farm; more than an hour away from work; made for a long and painful commute. Cass cranked up the radio, letting hard rock assault her eardrums. But the loud music didn't stop visions of her Dad with the green ball cap blown off his head. Blood dripping down his thick arms. Why couldn't the police find the scum-bastards who thought an addictive leaf was more valuable than her father's life? She gripped her steering wheel until her knuckles turned white. She couldn't let rage distract her from navigating the wet highway.

Cass pulled into her driveway and looked out at the sky. Was it clearing? The old farm house looked sunken and small, like it was also grieving the loss of Brad and Arlette. Sun broke through the clouds and she felt a bit of rare peace as the warm rays touched her cheek. She got out of her Subaru wagon and walked up the old wood steps through the front door. Navajo rugs added color to the small rooms and dated decor. Her mother had weaved them herself and were the most beautiful things in the house.

A big black pickup truck with rust on the side rattled into the driveway. Cass leaned out the front door and shouted at the tall skinny man who climbed out of the cab.

"Let's have a picnic! I think it might actually be a clear evening."

"Love of my life, anything for you" Devon said, "just let me change."

He gave Cass a kiss on the cheek and dropped his yellow work overalls by her backpack. She went into the kitchen to make a basket of bologna, processed cheese, and rice cakes (pickings were slim at the grocery store). Devon lived with his parents up the road on a beef cattle farm. His day job was taking care of all the public park trees, keeping them trimmed and healthy. They'd been casually dating for a couple of years, but after Brad Smudge was murdered, he came by with flowers, beef pies, and a suitcase.

"I was going to propose before living together, but no way I'm leaving you alone now. The ring can come later," he'd said.

She went out to his truck and put a couple quilts in the cargo bed then went back for the food. Devon, in jeans and a clean shirt, grabbed the picnic basket from her.

"Did you call the cops again today?" He asked as they drove to the back of the field where the view was most spectacular. Cass's farm had a huge berm of cedar trees planted along the road for soil erosion. The barrier was also great for privacy. Devon had brought over some of his Angus cows to eat the corn left in the field. Almost no local farmer had bothered combining the rain-stunted silage. The black beasts scattered as the four-wheel drive tore through the mud.

"Yes. Still nothing," she gestured to the bucking cattle. "I can't believe people are trying to steal your cows off your family farm. At least you can't see them from the road here. Plus, the standing corn isn't going to waste."

Devon smiled at her and parked on the highest point of the land. Both of them hopped into the back of the pickup truck. The view was spectacular. Pine trees and farm fields rolling as far as the eyes could see.

Cass reached into her wicker picnic basket and passed her boyfriend a beer.

"I found one of those green bugs in my backpack. Are they still spreading in the region?"

"Well, I saw some oak trees that didn't look so good. Trees are dying faster than we can plant them."

Cass took a sip of her drink, "and no one can identify them yet?"

"I bagged one of the buggers to send off to Pest Control Canada. But I figure it's a new invasive species."

"Just what we need, another evil breed of bug," Cass took a cheese slice from the basket.

They ate and laid back on the blankets in companionable silence as the sky got darker. A few light trails shot across the sky.

"Did you see that! Was there supposed to be a meteor shower tonight?" Devon sat up quickly.

"Looks like it landed in the next field," Cass said.

"Well, we don't want to be conked on the head by a rock," Devon joked, "Let's head back."

Cass noticed a glow coming from the other side of the field, "Why are the grow lights on in the greenhouse? I told you to stay out of there!"

"I'm getting tired of eating rice cakes babe. Your dad's greenhouse is enormous. We could feed a family of eight for a year," Devon's face reddened as his voice rose.

"I'd rather starve. It's full of bad memories," she clenched her fists.

"Look, I wanna test a theory. I've noticed when I add more LED lights, the bugs scatter. I'm planting fruit and vegetables. Kale, cucumbers, tomatoes, beans, and strawberries."

"I swore I would never go back in there," she softened a little.

She went to bed hungry every night. Her favorite jeans were swimming on her. Cass's mouth salivated at the idea of fresh strawberries. The produce section was bare at the market. Arlette had taught her to make amazing strawberry pies, and she could sell them at the road side, or give them away to hungry families.

"Whatever, do you what you need to do," she muttered as they drove back up to the house.

She didn't wake Devon up in the morning, quickly getting dressed and heading out the door. Normally she gave him a kiss, and but he had kept her up till midnight talking about his plans for the cursed greenhouse. She kept seeing her father's bloody body, murdered for a plant. She plotted revenge instead of sleeping.

In the morning, she could swear she saw even more bugs than usual inching along the battered corn stalks, but it was hard to tell in the dim early morning light.

Cass drove exhausted to the city with waves of rain beating against the windshield. Last night's clear skies seemed a dream. The slicing of the wipers was so loud she couldn't even hear her rock music. The highway ditch was littered with hydroplaned cars, but she managed to get to work safely before the real rush-hour. Arriving early worked in Cass's favor to find a premium outdoor parking spot. The underground parking lot was flooded.

She turned on her computer and the first story she had to write was depressing. Farmers committing suicide at an alarming rate. The piece explained crop failure, low yields and financial troubles were to blame. Cass tapped out quickly:

Why are our farmers dying?

Short and dramatic, good for "click through." Some of her co-workers had been laid off as the economy slid into a depression, but the Farm website was growing in popularity. The public was trying to understand why they couldn't buy fresh vegetables and food banks were running out of food. She looked out her window at the new sign posted on the flooded loading dock of The Sugar Factory.

Redpath is closed until further notice due to high water levels.

Cass noticed another green bug crawling on her desk. Instead of trying to smush it, she let it crawl onto her palm. A vision of her father tied in a chair, a man pointing a gun at him. She recognized the mutton chops and scarred face. Her neighbor Carl. She watched, horrified, as he fired. Her vision washed out in a sea of red.

Gasping she dropped the bug and charged out of the building. The drive home a blur as she kept seeing Carl shooting her father. Both men giants. The blood splashing onto the leaf she's watching from.

Pulling into her driveway, the downpour exhausted itself into a persistent drizzle. She didn't notice the black pickup truck in the driveway. Devon intercepted her mad dash down the hall with the tractor keys in his hand.

"What are you doing home?" She asked.

"My hours have been cut back, so I'm working in the greenhouse."

She yanked the keys out of his hands, "We have to go over to Carl's right now! I think he murdered Dad."

"Slow down. Why would an old wanna-be biker kill Brad Smudge?"

"Just come!"

Devon and Cass crossed the country concession from the far edge of their land to pass onto Carl's land surreptitiously. He had a few Buffalo grazing his hay field with chain link fencing and signs posted every few feet.

Danger. Keep Out. Buffalo Pasture.

They clambered over the fence, and dropped onto the grass.

"Sssh," Devon said gesturing to a bull sleeping in the grass several feet away. His heavy head rested on the ground while his long damp fur stuck to the sides of his enormous torso. Long tapered horns framed the wide head. They walked quickly by him, the creature not even stirring. Two other buffalo, smaller than the bull, were at the back of the paddock, heads down nipping up alfalfa.

"What kind of Buffalo business survives with a herd of three?" Cass asked.

"A front organization, that's what kind," Devon said, his tall frame hunched as he ran along the edge of the fencing.

At the back of Carl's property, there was a small stable and riding arena. It had seen better days, the paint peeling off the barn board. Trees surrounded the building, old oak and walnut half dead, and a back driveway accessed the cavernous riding area. A few Harleys, in far better shape than Carl's, were parked near the roll-up door.

"Maybe Carl isn't such a wanna be after all," Devon crept up to an oil-streaked window.

Cass followed him and they peered into the arena. There were rows and rows of green plants hanging upside down in the ring. Wire was strung from one end of the 70' by 130' foot space to the other. A couple of rough looking men in leather jackets with some sort of patch on them were sitting in lawn chairs in the corner.

"Can you read the patch?" Cass asked, her face flushing with anger, "They must have killed my dad for his pot. They aren't growing it. Just drying and selling it."

"We don't need to know which biker gang did this, let's get out of here and call the cops," Devon put a hand on Cass's back and hustled her through the buffalo paddock.

"Devon. I think one of those strange bugs telepathically showed me Dad getting shot," tears gathered in her eyes and there was a strange sensation in her stomach. She didn't know if it was relief, anger, or nausea.

"Really? Maybe those bugs could be useful after all," he ran faster.

The large bull was awake and grazing when they scuttled by, but he ignored them. Jumping up onto the fence, the both of them clambered over, ran across the road, and flew into the farm house.

Cass pulled her cell phone out of her pocket. She called 911and reported the illegal operation across the road and her suspicions about the death of her father. She didn't mention telepathic bugs. Devon went out into the struggling corn field and came back fifteen minutes later with two of the beetles in a mason jar.

They both cupped one in their hands. The little legs tickled Cass's hands as she felt the creature exploring her palm. No panic or attempt to escape. The same vision of a dune-filled landscape, with dead bent trees. She held the bug longer this time. Two moons were in the sky, and strange rock formations could be seen in the distance.

She opened her eyes and looked at Devon, sliding the bug back into the jar.

"What did you see?" she asked.

Devon also placed his bug back and closed the lid. The two green creatures roamed around the bottom of it, tentacles exploring the glass.

"I think I saw the prairies, but all the crops were gone. Just dirt and bugs everywhere,"

"I saw something similar, but I don't think it was on earth. It was like a planet that'd been completely devoured by bugs."

They stared at each other, as sirens in the distance grew closer.

6 MONTHS LATER

Cass flicked on the news to get an update on the state of the world.

"Global flooding is the worst it has ever been. The constant rain has helped the "Yama Bug," as scientists have dubbed it, decimate our crops."

She clicked to another channel

"India is in crisis and the people are rioting, famine is a reality…"

Click

"Food insecurity in the United States had led to civil unrest in the streets…"

Click

"The Yama Bug, coined after the Hindu god of death, and we don't know where the species originated from. Pesticides don't kill them…

She turned off the television and turned to Devon.

"It this how we go? Humanity gets taken out by the Bug Age?" Cass asked.

She looked out the window where a green beetle probed the glass with long tentacles. It looked perfectly content bathing in the sheets of rain lashing the house. Devon hiked around the property every morning and had some favorite bugs he visited. He would give them a quick touch to see if anyone was casing their farm. It took practice, but the both of them were learning how to tap into the beetle's telepathy.

He had been laid off completely from his arborist job, but Devon was still writing her headlines (and even articles now) from home. As long as the power was still on, people wanted to keep tabs on agricultural news.

"If we can learn to work with the bugs, maybe the rest of the world can," Devon pulled on his rain coat.

Cass slipped into galoshes and followed him out the door. The two of them walked to the back of the property where her father's greenhouse sat, glowing with the extra generator-powered lights. There was a river at the back of the property and her boyfriend had figured out how to tap the water's energy to run his generator. She followed Devon in through the door and breathed deeply. The smell of fresh tomatoes, cucumbers and strawberries filled her lungs.

She could finally handle being in the place her dad died.

The bikers were convicted of drug trafficking, and Carl jailed for the murder of Brad Smudge. Carl had been the president of "Satan's Sinners", a small local biker gang, and the police found many weapons hidden in his barn, including the murder weapon. Carl's oily finger prints all over the rifle that killed her father. The bug's vision had been bang-on.

She took out her iPhone and filmed Devon working on his plants and replacing LED bulbs. They had started up their own farming YouTube channel, called "Survive the Yama". They were teaching families how to grow enough food in small greenhouses to last them at least a year. So far, having enough light seemed the best way to fight the beetles. They didn't like the sun, bright light, or LED grow bulbs. Scientists were working around the clock figuring out how to disperse the cloud cover and let sunlight bathe the planet again. So many people were watching Cass and Devon's videos, they sometimes crashed the site.

When she got enough footage, she pressed her nose up against the glass to look outside. She was finally a film maker and she silently thanked Brad Smudge for this greenhouse. It was their only hope for survival until they could figure out how to either stop the Yama beetle, or co-exist with them. So far, they had proven to be wonderful sentries. The world needed better communication. Perhaps telepathy was the answer?

She shuddered thinking about the dreadful dead landscapes in her early visions from the bugs. In the darkening evening she saw the bright glow of another meteor catapulting to earth. It tore a beautiful line of light through the cloudy sky.

What she didn't see were the thousands of green bugs nestled within the silicon, iron and nickel of the space rocks.

23

ABOUT "CLINT CHESTER CONFECTIONARY"

~

$\mathcal{A}$n Original Story for Peculiar Pets

Jade C. Wildy is a guest author in this collection, and her candy shop has an unusual clientele...

Jade C. Wildy writes speculative fiction on themes like death, psychological state, and being different. She delights in slipping in the unexpected. Her writing is featured in numerous publications across the world. A self-confessed wallflower, she lives on Kaurna Lands in Australia and can frequently be found writing or drawing in the local cafes. www.jadewildywordsmith.com

24

CLINT CHESTER CONFECTIONARY

BY JADE C. WILDY

~

When Clint Chester Windchester lay dazed and bleeding on the side of the M23 next to what had previously been his motorbike (now a tangled mess of scrap metal), three rather unexpected, yet significant things occurred to him. The first was that his encounter with a lorry, which was on the wrong side of the motorway, probably should have left him dead. He had definitely seen the white light and heard the willowy music (probably inspired by Enya) but decided it wasn't for him.

Yet, having decided to live, thoughts of the afterlife faded quickly from Clint's mind, to be replaced by the second significant thing. He didn't want to sell diet supplements. Perhaps it was because his motorcycle-scrapping accident had happened on the way to work, but he felt it far more likely his brush with death made him realise he didn't want a career duping people into feeling bad about themselves in order to sell weight-loss products. They didn't actually work anyway (which, of course, was the dieter's fault, and definitely not because failure kept customers walking through the doors!). No. Clint didn't want any part of that any more. He wanted to make candy.

BY JADE C. WILDY

The third epiphany was that there was, undeniably, both good and bad at play in the world. Clint knew this because as he was trundled into the back of an ambulance to be taken to the extremely expensive Good Sisters of Undeniable Charity Hospital, both Good and Bad were there with him. Not in a metaphorical sense, but in the form of two small, talking dogs who were arguing over how many tongue depressors it was acceptable to steal. Bad, a skinny creature with the appearance of a mohawked terrier with buck teeth bore a striking resemblance to his great-grandmother's dog, Penny, and argued it should be "All of them." While Good, a plump little labrador puppy with golden ringlet hair, of the type to inspire people to sing "How Much is that Doggy in the Window?", said, "None of them" (or at least a maximum of three).

Why did they look that way? Who knew. Clint assumed it was some kind of subconscious sense of what 'Good' and 'Bad' should look like, and he did have strong feelings about dogs (especially his great-grandmother's ghastly terrier), despite never having had the pleasure of one's company. God and Bad had been his constant companions ever since, helping him through the legal loopholes of his employer trying to invoice him for quitting his job, the establishment of his confectionary shop, and watching every football match to occur in the intervening years. Clint didn't recall ever getting a TV license for it, but Good was oddly quiet on the matter, so Clint let it go.

Today, Good was brooding. They sat upon the edge of a pound box of toffee gems, tail curled around their legs, staring glumly at the speckled pattern their pawprints had made in the scattered icing sugar. Clint suspected it was because Emily, a sweet child who wore a blue satin bow in her hair and a smile on her dimpled face, had not visited Clint Chester Confectionary in quite a while. Emily was one of Good's favorites, but Clint didn't half wonder if the child had perhaps... moved on.

He looked over at Bad. Bad was making fondant flowers, their little brow furrowed in a parody of human concentration as they nudged at the dough with their nose like they were burying something. Clint made a note to check them later but decided it was best to leave Bad alone as well. Not just because Bad was concentrating, but because he didn't want Bad to start bugging Good. Even Good would bark and nip when pressed, which Bad had a characteristically bad habit of doing.

At that moment, a slight, uncanny breeze stirred the sweet air of the candy shop and the outside doorbell rang. Good's head shot up as the door cracked open, but instead of Emily, the gaunt figure of Mr. Mortimer Graves stepped through. As always, he was wearing a smart, if dated, black suit - the kind people were buried in.

Bad put down the crinkly-edged pink peony they had been working on to greet Mr. Graves with a yip and a saluted paw. Bad, for whatever reason, liked Mr. Graves.

"Good afternoon." Mr. Graves nodded in response to Bad. "Might I purchase a small box of wiffle taffy?" His deep voice gave the impression of an old-school headmaster from the 1970s, or perhaps a tax accountant. Definitely, someone who made other people miserable. Certainly, *not* someone who could stereotypically be seen as a person who would buy wiffle taffy. Yet, there they all were.

Good slowly moved off the box of gems to fetch the wiffles from their cabinet, and place them in a little purpose-made box.

"Just the three?" they called over their shoulder, carefully ensuring each was equally spaced with a dainty pat of their little paw.

"Just the three," Mr Graves agreed. He turned to Clint and leaned a long, bony arm on the counter.

"My dear boy, how has business been this week?" It was always a curious thing that he asked since nothing about the man suggested he was the type to voluntarily make small talk.

"Business is good," Clint told him. "I expect things will get busy shortly, once school lets out."

Good appeared beside them, carrying the wiffle taffy box, now tied with a yellow bow. They set it down in front of Mr. Graves and gave Bad a wary glare.

Mr. Graves picked up the small box. "Many thanks." He nodded and left with the same uncanny breeze that had struck up as he arrived.

One may think it odd that Mr. Graves could not only see Good and Bad, accepted their canine appearance, and interacted with them since they were generally invisible to anyone except Clint, *and* that he had left without paying. However, Mr. Graves was one of Clint Chester Confectionery's special customers.

Clint picked up the now soulless box of wiffle taffy - all the flavor had now left it - and placed it in the bin. He reminded himself that the dead were people too and should be treated with respect, even if it meant binning wiffle taffy, particularly since Clint had nearly ended up among them all those years ago. Even Bad wasn't going to argue with Clint on that one.

The bell rang again, and Clint looked up to find, as predicted, a gaggle of school kids, oozing through the door with every ounce of cool they could muster, in as much as they were buying sweets (Or, as was more often the case, stealing). These substantially more alive customers could not see Good nor Bad, either in a metaphorical sense —or the little dogs that were now making their way out into the shopfront. Clint leaned on the counter to watch his invisible companions go to work.

A girl with freckles was standing on the other side of the storefront near the soda fridges. She was being heckled into putting a bottle of Clint's handcrafted strawberry soda into her bag by two of her friends under the influence of Bad. Good, however, was working furiously on the girl to stand up to the pressure of her peers. With a stab, Clint thought Bad had won this round as the girl abruptly snatched the bottle from her friend's grasp. Yet, instead of placing it in her bag, she turned and, giving her friends a sour look, paid Clint for the soda then returned to her companions.

"He's just trying to make a living. Don't be jerks," she hissed at the other two as they left. It is sometimes hard to do what you know to be the right thing when the disappointment your friends express suggests it's somehow the wrong thing. Without even looking, Clint could sense the chest swelling, puff of pride in Good, that the girl hadn't given in to her friends. However, Good's work wasn't finished (was it ever?). On seeing the looming loss of the Strawberry Soda Pop Battle, Bad had gone to work on the other students scattered around the room.

A mixed bunch of youths crowded around the tubs of assorted bulk sweets to block Clint's view from the one or two that were shoving fistfuls of individually wrapped candy and chocolates into their blazer pockets. He had seen Bad encourage this particular tactic before. Remarkably, and somewhat irritatingly, Good wasn't in *their* ears. Clint sighed and walked over to them.

"A fistful is about 250g of lollies. You can pay per pocket and save the bag, or admit you got busted and chuck them back." Clint stood over them with his arms crossed over his chest.

With some grumbling and grunting, the sweets were thrown back into the tubs. Unfortunately, one awkward lad misjudged his throw and the sweets went cascading to the floor. The gaggle of youths decided to bolt rather than clean up the mess, except the one that had thrown the candy. He didn't quite manage to make his exit before Clint blocked the door. Bad chuckled on the hapless boy's shoulder as Clint oversaw him sweeping them up.

The last of the school ratbags were sauntering out when a great yelp came from the counter. Clint turned to see a lad with close-cropped hair and the poise and pedigree that spoke of affluence trying to remove his hand from Clint's open till where it had somehow become inexplicably stuck. Good sat atop the till, the tip of their tail twitching in an almost suppressed wag. Clint stifled a laugh.

"It seems your mates have left you to your fate," he told the lad, whose eyes streamed with tears as he desperately tried to free his fingers. "Perhaps try letting go of the money."

The boy looked stricken as he relinquished his grip on the numerous notes, and the till in turn released his fingers. "I wasn't trying to steal anything."

"You really don't expect me to believe that?" Clint scoffed. It was an impressive lie, given the swot was literally caught with his hand in the til. Clint shot a glance at Bad. Their innocent puppy-dog eyes suggested they certainly had a role in the lie.

"You can't prove anything." The youth then had the audacity to give Clint the dented finger. At that moment, the seam on the boy's jacket decided it wasn't worth holding on anymore, and his pocket split. Sweets burst forth like Guy Fawkes Fireworks, followed by a fat wallet and mobile phone that made a satisfying thwack sound as it hit the floor.

"I guess that didn't happen either?" Clint remarked. Behind him, Bad snorted.

The lad looked decidedly sheepish. "Fine." He sighed, took a note from the impressive collection in his wallet and dumped it on the counter. "Keep the change," he said as he sauntered out as haughtily as he could muster while sucking at his fingers like a tired toddler.

"A spontaneously jamming till and weak pocket seams punishes the wicked? How very savage of you, Good!" Bad said, tail thumping as they let out a cackling, evil laugh.

"Universal Karma," Good muttered.

"Those children were awful." A small voice came from the other side of the counter. "They should be far nicer in the only lolly shop still open after the bombs came down." Good leapt and zoomied across the counter as quickly as their little divine legs would carry them. Emily had finally appeared.

The little girl wore her hair in long braids and a grey pinafore, over a white cotton dress that looked too big for her. A well-loved, if battered, hand-made doll was clutched under one arm.

"Ah, Emily," Good told the little girl. "You're quite right. Not one of them holds a candle to the goodness you possess."

Bad made loud retching sounds (the kind that usually struck fear into the hearts of those who owned both pets and carpets) at the other side of the counter, earning himself a gentle, if firm, flick from Clint, who had begun to sweep up the sea of confectionary that still littered the shop floor. The little girl tittered.

"How are things with you, Emily?" Clint asked, leaning on his broom. "We haven't seen you for a while." He looked over the collection of sweets on the counter, wondering which Emily might enjoy.

"Mama says Papa should be with us any day now, and then we will be moving to the country." The little girl beamed. "I've never been to the country. Not with the war and all."

"Oh, it sounds delightful, my dear-" Good started.

"If you like that sort of thing," Bad interrupted.

"But I certainly shall miss your company!" Good's tail swung wildly. "Perhaps some chocolate-covered Turkish Delight for a delightful girl?"

"I swapped that out for apricot," Bad hissed.

"I know," Good hissed back.

Clint chuckled, scooped a load of the chocolates into a pink bag, and handed them to Emily. She was such a sweet-mannered child.

"Must dash. Mama doesn't like it if I'm away too long." Emily took her bag and skipped out of the door into the uncanny breeze. Clint had never seen the little girl's mother in all the years the child had been appearing at the *Clint Chester Confectionery* shop to buy sweets. It was a peculiar fact that the dead didn't seem to know they had died. He picked up the now soulless chocolate bag and regarded the door the little girl ghost had left by.

"What do we think?" Clint asked his strange companions.

"Probably had a bomb dropped on them." Good looked sadly towards the door, his tail now hanging limp. "There were quite a few that flattened this whole area." The World War II history of the town was well-known. It had been almost entirely destroyed early in the conflict.

"And dear old Dad was likely off soldiering and survived." Bad sniffed at the soulless bag, then sneezed on the counter. "He's probably in some hospital right now, about to snuff it from old age."

Sadness was Clint's first response. It was a hangover from before his motorcycle accident, coming from the thought of people becoming dearly departed at the end, never to be seen again. Now he knew better, but whatever came after the dearly departed, actually departed was still a mystery to him, so he was a little conflicted.

Good was watching him. "They've probably waited a very long time to see each other again." They sighed deeply. "Bittersweet."

A racket started up behind them in the workshop behind the counter, breaking into the maudlin moment. Bad had turned on the telly. Good made a mock snarl and biting motion completely inconsistent with who, or perhaps what they were supposed to represent.

"We were having a moment, Bad!" Good yelled.

"Have it on your own time!" Bad shouted back. "We missed the start of the game."

"Oh, Lord!" Good scrambled from the counter to the work table, to curl up on a small bench carefully crafted from no more than three tongue depressor sticks, which gave an excellent view of the telly. Bad scooted over to make room for them.

"Ow! We are already down, two-nil." Bad passed Good a bowl of popcorn that had miraculously appeared.

Clint wondered if these two dog-shaped entities were taking liberties with divine intervention, but swept the thought aside as the two consciences cheered the sudden failure of the opposition goalie. What peculiar quirk was it that made his consciences more concerned with football than almost anything else on Earth - so much so that they didn't acknowledge the gust of uncanny wind, nor the doorbell. Clint dragged his eyes off the game to greet the late customer.

"Twice in one day Mr. Graves?" Clint smiled at the gaunt man. "To what do I owe the pleasure?"

"I noticed little Emily had a bag of chocolates that I don't believe I have sampled." Mr. Graves smiled politely. "Who is winning?" He nodded to the ruckus on the screen. A slew of profanities suddenly erupted out of Bad's mouth, the gist of which was an awarded penalty.

Good leapt up at the same time. "Kick him in the PANTS!" Good growled, the fur at their neck spiked in hackled frustration. Clint, Bad, and Mr. Graves stared at them in surprise. "What? Ump deserves it for a call like that." Good sat back down again, yet continued to emit low growls every time the umpire appeared on the screen. Even Bad cocked their head at Good.

"You do keep some unusual company, Master Winchester." Mr. Graves smiled politely.

"Dead right!" Bad laughed, before they were hurriedly hushed by Good. It wasn't clear if there was any etiquette about pointing out the deads'... deadness, but Clint agreed with Good that it certainly didn't seem polite, especially if the dead themselves weren't aware. It certainly wasn't nice to make jokes at their expense.

"I wouldn't change the company in my shop for anything," Clint told Mr. Graves, handing over the bag of chocolates from a box that now said "Apeish Delight."

Mr. Graves paused in the doorway, the chocolate bag clasped in his long, spidery fingers, and turned to Clint. "I do know that I am no longer living," he said, quietly. "But I spent so much time in life doing what was expected, I missed out on a lot of good things that were unexpected." He slightly jostled the chocolate bag. "I can't risk the afterlife being as expected until I have enjoyed the unexpected here. So, my thanks, Clint Chester Windchester, you are lucky to have done the unexpected when you were still around to enjoy it." He gestured with a single finger to the confectionary shop around them, bowed, and quietly left.

Good and Bad had torn their focus of the game to stare at the closed door.

Good looked up at Clint. "How perfectly extraordinary. I thought all the ghosts were oblivious to their dead status."

"Unexpected isn't it?" Clint winked at Good.

Bad let out a deep groan. "I can't believe you just..." They shook their head and returned to berating the umpires.

Clint considered the two strange, talking dogs now barking loudly at the television, then looked down at his hands. That day on the motorway he had expected to die. He had questioned the things he did, realized he came up lacking by his own values, and decided to do some things no one expected: he had decided he would live, and that he would make candy. The thought stirred in the back of his mind as he sat among the boiled lollies, sherbert, and fudge that perhaps he *hadn't* achieved one of those things, at least not completely, but Clint decided it didn't matter. He was doing what he enjoyed and was able to do a little good and fend off a little bad in the world. At least the customers were interesting.

25

ABOUT "WHY RIDE A BROOM?"

~

First published: January 2022
Dark Dispatch

THIS CHARACTER SKIT *features a man abracadabra-ed into a horse by a witch. A cautionary tale for those who think there are no consequences for rude behavior.*

26

———

WHY RIDE A BROOM

BY ANGELIQUE FAWNS

$\mathcal{B}$eing a recently gelded Paint horse with fine black and white patches isn't what makes me unique. What makes me unique is that I'm a man trapped in this equine body. At least, I used to be a man. Now I guess I'm what's called a Eunuch. Date one wrong broad, and I'm condemned to prancing around in leather gear and munching on old dry grass. How was I to know Karen was a witch? I should have known better than to use the dating app *Earth Mothers & Mates*.

My buddy told me about it, how the ratio of men to women is completely in our favour. Using the usual on-line sites means millions of men basically begging the ladies to swipe right. He said the women were begging for men to maul them on this new dating app. So did I ever get to swiping. Now, with hooves, all I can swipe at are the shavings in this wood cell. I used to like being on top, but she wanders down to the stables whenever she wants, rides me hard, and puts me away wet.

"There's my sweet little patchy twat," she says while shoving an apple between my lips.

I neigh and nip at her, but she just giggles and dances away, sliding the bolt shut on my stall. I nicker desperately, willing Karen to

125

come back. At least when she's here, I feel safe. There is a big orange horse beside me, a chestnut mare, and she bares her teeth at me with her ears pinned flat against her head. I'm convinced she's going to kick through my stall and trample me to death one of these nights.

I thought I had scored when I first saw Karen's profile on Earth Mothers & Mates. Long black hair to her butt, great bod, she looked like a go-er. So how was I to know that she was super-sensitive? We had a great date. I took her to my favorite pub because the hockey game was on. I let her order any beer that was on tap. Shoved a bunch of wings down her throat and then took her back home. It was a great time.

So, when we went back to her place, she invited me in for a nightcap. Hey, we all know what that means. The lady was looking for love. There were candles and shit burning everywhere, ambiance am I right? I'm a good-looking dude. I mean when I wasn't a black and white horse with manure stains on my rump. Tall, dark-haired ... good bod from pumping the iron. We had our drinks and she only had wine, so I got a glass down, though I'm a brew guy. Then it got all romantical. She was a pretty good lay. Curvy in all the right places, know what I'm saying?

But then she wanted to know what we were doing together tomorrow night, and I had to let her know I was the "here for a good time, not a long time" kinda guy. Well, Karen didn't like that one bit. She got a bit hot under the collar and not the way I usually like it. Telling me she's a lady and I had to learn to be a gentleman. Then ala kazaam. I'm a horse. Then before you know it, she's called a vet ... my god, I can't even tell you about that.

I think it's been a week since that night? Hard to gauge time because I sleep so much. Who knew napping could be so fulfilling, and it's not like I got to go to the office, am I right? Someone else is selling those used cars. I've got a favorite place in the paddock under a big oak tree. Thank goodness that red bitch of a mare is in a different field. They keep the geldings (or ball-less boys as we all are) together when we're let out to kick our heels up for the day.

Karen has great hands. I do enjoy it when she uses her soft brush and grooms my coat. I twist my neck in the air and flap my lips when she hits the best spots. But then I remember she trapped me in this horse body, and stole my nuts. Then I lift my leg to kick her, but she gives my nose a pinch and I put it down.

I've thought about jumping the fence of my paddock and high-tailing for the hills. But where would I go? And what if the red horse followed me? I don't ever want to be alone with the chestnut mare in the next stall. Maybe life here isn't so bad. A truck just pulled up with a whole load of carrots, and they smell delish. I used to joke that I wished I could find a woman who was into leather and whips. Guess now I found one.

ABOUT THE AUTHOR

Angelique Fawns loves to spin dark tales and is incredibly nosy. She takes her natural inclination to ask far too many questions and interviews publishers, editors, and authors for horrortree.com and her own blog at www.fawns.ca/blog.

She has a day job as a television producer and lives on a farm north of Toronto with her husband, daughter, horses, cats, and a rescued Potcake dog.

When she can find the time, she sneaks away to her Golden Falcon trailer by the river to do some writing. You can find her work in *Ellery Queen Mystery Magazine*, *DreamForge*, *& Stupefying Stories* to name a few.

facebook.com/amfawns
x.com/angeliquefawns
instagram.com/angeliqueiswriting

BUT WAIT! THERE'S MORE.

Enjoyed this book? Check out the others in the Horror Lite Series!

Cursed & Creepy

Mythical Monsters

Like to listen?

Read Me A Nightmare Podcast

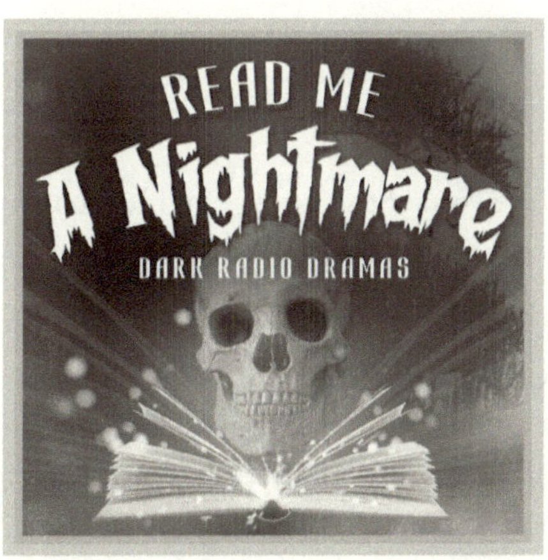

Did you enjoy reading these dark quirky tales? Would you like to hear them performed on a podcast? Look for *Read Me A Nightmare* wherever you get your podcasts.

A writer yourself?

The Guide of All Guides

To learn more about selling your short stories and making money, I've created a guide to the best no-fee paying markets.

The Guide of All Guides is a comprehensive list of publishers and podcasters buying speculative fiction, complete with secrets and insights. Newly updated as of November 2023!

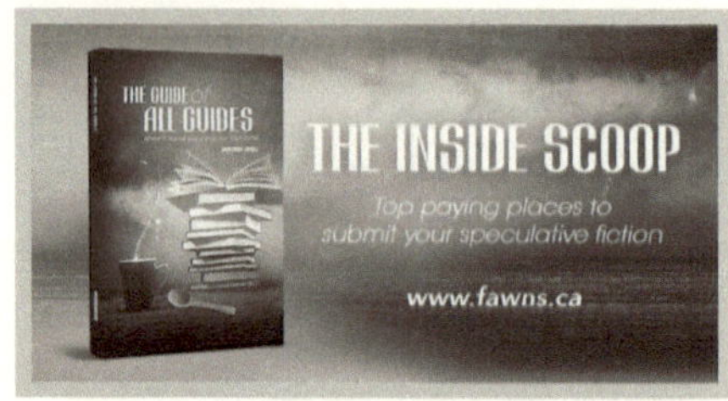

****Sign Up for my newsletter at www.fawns.ca*

If you enjoyed the foreword of this book, I highly recommend you check out Mark Leslie's **Superstitious: A Fiction River Anthology.**

https://books2read.com/superstitious

Superstitions pervade every culture and belief system. Often, the origins of such superstitions elude their practitioners. The seventeen authors in this latest volume of Fiction River create their own superstitious tales in fascinating stories ranging from dark and moody to light and fun, from introspective and thought-provoking to high-ratcheted tension.